BOY FROM THE BUILDING SITE

Charlie Parkes

Copyright © 2023 Charles Parkes

All rights reserved

The characters and events portrayed in this book are fictitious. Any similarity to real persons, living or dead, is coincidental and not intended by the author.

No part of this book may be reproduced, or stored in a retrieval system, or transmitted in any form or by any means, electronic, mechanical, photocopying, recording, or otherwise, without express written permission of the publisher.

ISBN: 9798396319363
Imprint: Independently published

Cover design by: Art Painter
Library of Congress Control Number: 2018675309
Printed in the United States of America

To Charlotte and William, our grandchildren who bring so much joy, song, dance, laughter and football into our lives.

To Neal Harrison for providing the inspiration for this story.

In fond memory of Archy Armour - my childhood playmate

"Indulge your imagination in every possible flight."

JANE AUSTEN

CONTENTS

Title Page
Copyright
Dedication
Dedication
Epigraph
Our first home   2
My Gang   16
Fun and games   25
Holidays   29
Walters and Armour - Private Investigators   47
School   59
Romeo and Julia   70
Daylight robbery   83
UXBs   96
New house, New home.   106
Shenanigans in the park   114
The Interview   123
Photographs   136
About The Author   138

CHARLIE PARKES

OUR FIRST HOME

I am William Walters, sometimes known as Fred as you will find out later. Me Dad was a Scouser. James "Jimmy" Walters. Me Mam was Veronica but always known as Vee, and she came from Chesterfield in Derbyshire, the town with the wonky spire. Grandma and Granddad had a corner shop there, an offie or off licence selling drink and tobacco but also newspapers and a range of essential items.

Crooked Spire Chesterfield

Dad was a joiner leaving school at 14 to be an apprentice for a local builder. That was in 1939 during World War Two that left many shattered buildings and lives, and there was a lot of work to do shoring up bombed buildings or just demolishing them. Any road up, when he got to be eighteen he decided to join up at the recruiting office in a local drill hall. His skills at building and demolition were immediately recognised and within a couple of weeks, he was a Sapper in the Royal Engineers. Sappers are military combat engineers and tradesmen and their history goes back to the 17th century, when attackers dug covered trenches to approach the walls of a besieged fort.

James "Jimmy" Walters

After a test to identify his Army trade he went on basic training, had a few days leave and joined his unit. Soon after, he was shipped to a tented camp near Southampton to be kitted out with equipment including a 25lb explosive charge on top of his normal pack. He was about to be part of Operation Overlord, D Day, the invasion of Europe. Thousands of men on hundreds of ships set sail down the Solent past the Isle of Wight with a piper playing them off from the shore of Osborne House, but then the boats turned back because of the rough sea and bad weather. They went again the next day and this time he landed on the beaches. So if anyone asked him what he did in the war he would just say "Built some things and blew others up." He went across France supporting infantry building Bailey bridges, dealing with booby traps and land mines, laying telephone cables and anything the infantry needed.

After the war, he was demobilised along with five million service personnel, returning home to life in civvy street with a lot of memories,* a demobilisation grant and a set of civilian clothing, including the so-called "demob suit", shirts, underclothes, raincoats, hat, shoes and a suitcase. Rationing would continue until 1954 so there remained a shortage of many of the basic essentials of living including food, clothing, and housing. Husbands and wives also had to adjust to living together. The country was short of manpower so all able-bodied men were required to report to the Ministry of Labour to be allocated a job. Me Dad didn't want any old job and returned to his old trade as a qualified joiner, now with experience in engineering and explosives.

There was plenty of work building "temporary" pre-fabricated single storey houses known as pre-fabs for the poor souls bombed out of their homes. There was also a promise to provide "Homes fit for Heroes" resulting in council or social housing as it is now known. However, there was a lot of work rebuilding infrastructure, bridges, factories and docks that suited his skills and his pay packet so he joined a major construction company and travelled the country following the work. Eventually he arrived in Chesterfield living in digs [lodgings] with three other blokes from his site.

Pre-fabs

Every morning he walked across the street to Vee's offie for Golden Virginia tobacco, a box of Swans [matches], Rizla rolling papers and a newspaper. He kept his baccy, papers and ready-rolled fags in a St Bruno flake pipe tobacco tin. Inevitably a relationship developed with Vee, starting with a drink in the pub, the flicks, dancing and so it was that accidents may happen and I was about to appear on the scene. A visit to the registry office made me legitimate when I was born a few months later. Dad moved into the shop and all three shared a bedroom. My first bed was the bottom drawer taken from a chest of drawers. The toilet was outside but at least we did not share it with neighbours and we had proper toilet paper from the shop instead of sheets of newspaper on a nail. Friday night was bath night after closing in a tin bath in the middle of the kitchen floor.

Grandparent's off-licence

Dad's job was coming to an end. I was nearly one so he worked away from home returning two or three weekends a month. Their only transport was me Mam's push bike so Dad found a BSA Gold Flash 650cc motor bike and sidecar and soon had it running "sweet as a nut." If his job was a long way off he would remove the sidecar then put it back on to take me and me Mam out for the day. Dad didn't have a crash helmet so just turned his cloth cap back to front so it would not blow off. Mam would sit in the sidecar holding me in her arms but as I got older she would sit on the pillion and I could then be a pilot flying my aeroplane in formation with Biggles Special Air Police just like on the radio and his books.

Dad asked for a job on a big site where he heard that some workers could live there in cabins and managed to get a coveted married living van. Moving into our new home was absolute luxury. I had my own room, our own inside toilet and a sit-in bath with a shower. Mam had her own kitchen and so I became the boy from the building site.

George Clelland and Bill Kirkham, a joiner and a brickie, founded the company in the thirties and certainly prospered with a string of major projects up and down the country. Dad's job was assured and the pay was good plus the free mobile home.

I think it was a bit of a shock for me Mam leaving the shop and her parents and landing on a building site amidst derelict properties. But, she loved the new home, the space, inside toilet and shower. Above all else, it was her home. The other married men soon knocked together a washhouse outside with a gas boiler, dolly tubs, possticks and washboards. A posstick was like a three-legged stool with a long pole rising from the centre of the "seat" and a cross-handle at the top. The ladies possed the washing, twisting and agitating the clothing to get the muck out just like a twin tub or automatic washing machine but they didn't come along until the seventies. After a lot of pushing and pummelling the ladies used large wooden tongs to drag the soapy garments into fresh water to be rinsed and then it was all hands to the mangle, a huge cast iron device with a large wheel turning cogs driving two wooden rollers squeezing the water out.
"Fred! Mind your fingers in them rollers!" Mam would shout. Sometimes too late!

The washhouse was next to the site tea bar, a rickety lean-to of timber and a tarpaulin with scaffold planks on blocks for makeshift benches. Morning, midday and afternoon
Mr. Simpkins would ring an old brass hand bell to say it was brew time. The Mams would boil water in a large aluminium, catering kettle that had evaded the wartime call up for metals to make Spitfires. It sat on a large gas ring and the contents filled an equally large teapot, usually 99 Tea from the Co-op. It had to be left to brew until it was brown and strong, served in mugs with plenty of

sugar and full cream milk.

"Make sure the spoon can stand up in it Fred." was the call, as I handed out the mugs of builder's brew.

Monday was washday and the Mams joined to look after the kids, make tea and scrub the clothes on the washboards with bars of soap. Mam would turn the radio on and they would sing and even dance to the latest songs. They earned some pin money by doing for the single men laundering pants, socks, vests and collarless shirts. It was a matter of luck that they got their own clothes back. Lines were strung between scaffold poles and lengths of two-by-one with notched ends became props lifting the wet clothes into the breeze. Woe betides any workman who started a fire or created clouds of dust.

Rationing continued long after the war until 1954 and the last food to come off ration was meat. Fish and chips were never rationed so Friday night was chip night all wrapped in old newspapers. Sometimes we ate in the van or on a warm summer evening, we all went to a park with a big pond where Dads and sons sailed their model yachts. I yearned for my own boat and eventually one sailed into my life on my birthday. Dad had made it from scrap off the site and mum made the sails on her hand Singer sewing machine. Mum took a basket lined with tea towels to keep our feast warm, I had a bottle of lemonade, a milk stout for her and a Guinness or pale ale for dad.

Grandma taught Mam to be a good cook. One of her signature dishes was a large cream, enamel stew pan sitting on the stove gently tenderising a cheap cut of meat with whatever vegetables were in season. There were no supermarkets bringing in fresh veg from around the world, no freezer nor even a fridge and microwaves hadn't been invented. She filled the van with a wonderful warm homely aroma and it would last for days eventually reduced to a soupy liquid mopped up with thick doorsteps of fresh white bread.

Some tea times she would send me to the chippy with a bowl and tea towel to go with whatever she had cooked, often a cheese and onion pie or steak and kidney if she could afford it. In the early days, wages did not stretch very far. Dad would come in on Friday teatime and put his wage packet on the table so Mam could divide it up to cover the weekly living costs and bills. She had a black cash tin decorated with red and gold bands hidden in a saucepan at the back of a kitchen cupboard. Inside was a lift out tray with several compartments and underneath she kept her Post Office book. She gave him pocket money for fags and a drink. We were lucky because some of the bloke's would blow nearly all their wages on drink before going home. One pub put free bread and cheese on the bar encouraging the patrons to stay long after work to drink, eat and spend the wives' housekeeping.

Saturday Mam would buy a good joint for Sunday. It was the best meal of the week. Roast beef and the trimmings. Our meal started with Yorkshire pudding and onion gravy to fill you up before you tucked into the meat.
Mam often made a fruit pie on a plate, twirling the plate on all the fingers of her left hand and trimming the overhanging pastry with a knife. Nothing was wasted and she rolled the trimmings into a sausage cut into three. Like sausage rolls without any sausage! When cooked it was served as an accompaniment to the main course. Waste not want not. A bit dry but there was plenty of gravy.

Traditionally Dad carved and served the roast. On Monday, he got a slice of beef in a triple-decker sandwich, two slices of bread and beef topped with a third slice spread with dripping, and some pickled onions dipped in sugar. We had bread and dripping. It was also washday so a quick and simple meal was in order. Cold beef with bubble and squeak, yesterday's leftover vegetables mixed together and fried.

Tuesday was cottage pie, the minced up remains of the joint

topped with mashed potato. If we had lamb then it was hotpot or shepherd's pie. Wednesday could be sausage, which used nearly all her housekeeping, so Thursday was always a meal I would dread. Tinned tomatoes in a dish topped with cheese, baked in the oven, and served with bread and butter. We did not have a fridge in those days and food went off quickly especially in hot weather, so any bits of green or mould on the cheese were sliced off and Granddad often said, "Eating a bit of muck never does you any harm."

Meat, cheese and butter were stored in a meat safe, a wooden box with small mesh panels to keep the flies out, and Mams did not worry about best before or use by dates, food did not come sealed in plastic packages from a supermarket, we bought everything from the local shops in brown paper bags.

I think Granddad was right about a bit of muck giving you immunity from diseases and allergies because we were seldom ill, apart from measles and chickenpox, of course. I remember either my friend Archy or me having chickenpox and our Mams made us play together so the other caught it and got immunity. If I was sick or had an upset tummy Mam would make me a bowl of pobs, that's hot milk, torn up pieces of white bread sprinkled with sugar, a comforting food that was easy to digest and settled the stomach.

I had most of the childhood diseases but not too badly having had all my jabs or inoculations. Quite often, it was no more than a rash and a couple of days feeling unwell. I recall being speckled red all over which must have been measles or perhaps German measles. Maybe I had both and Chickenpox was a bit itchy and uncomfortable. As a young teenager, I got mumps that can affect the glands in your neck or, for boys in the testicle. Standing and letting the affected part dangle was very painful confining me to bed until I got a "bag on a belt" truss to hold things in place.

My brain subconsciously stores visual memories as pictures that I am unaware of until something triggers the brain to retrieve it.

Unfortunately, I do not know what it has filed away and there is no index or search engine. I suppose it is like virtual reality and I can turn what I see into what I write. What I cannot see or do not know can be filled in with imagination.

One such example was my first visit to the dentist. Several milk teeth had fallen out and placed under my pillow for the tooth fairy but now I was in need of some fillings and extractions. Being my first visit, I didn't know what to expect but the dark foreboding exterior of a Victorian semi-detached house-come-surgery was sufficient to put the frighteners on me. Mam pulled a large knob in the wall that rang a bell, rather like the school handbell. Mr Hurst the dentist answered and seemed to be a kind, almost elderly gentleman. The stained glass front door lead to a dimly lit oak panelled hallway with a tiled floor smelling of disinfectant and growing fear.

Turning right through the first door we were now in the front room where blinds obscured the bay window adding to the gloom and impending doom. I literally climbed into the chair, rather like a barbers chair, and onto a booster seat. Mam sat on a stool at the side of me holding my hand in reassurance as I took in my surroundings and the strange equipment.

To my right was a small white bowl which I later learnt was to spit out all the blood and debris. I was particularly interested in the drill hanging above me like a preying mantis ready to devour its next meal. Me!

It was frightening because I did not know what it could do to my senseless mouth but fascinating in its construction of articulated, pivoting arms like a desk lamp but with pullies and drive belts.

The belts formed a continuous loop driven by an electric motor on the floor and connected to the mouthpiece of the Mantis at the other.

Suddenly I was dazzled by a huge lamp suspended from an articulated stand and I was tilted backwards in the chair as Mr. Hurst pumped a foot pedal raising me and the chair until we were face to face.

After probing all my teeth and documenting each one in dentist's code on a chart he whispered to Mam what he needed to do. Neither looked terribly happy as Mam nodded a reluctant approval while squeezing my hand. Mr. Hurst began his work in earnest, with a giant syringe he injected anaesthetic all round my mouth both sides top and bottom until my whole mouth, gums and lips were completely senseless and felt all rubbery.

With a nod to Mam he stamped the foot pedal. The mantis roared into life and I watched mesmerised as the belt ran round the pullies with a low-pitched "growling" that vibrated and resonated throughout my skull as it ground into my cavities.

There was some respite as I rinsed my mouth with a pink liquid and tried to spit through my rubbery lips into the bowl. Mam helped by wiping my lips and chin. Each of seven, yes seven cavities, were crammed with filling and I thought that was the end.

I was wrong! Continuing my exposure to dangerous animals I now saw the jaws of a giant sucker heading for my face and clamping itself firmly over my mouth and nose as he told me to breath deeply. I was now rendered unconscious by the general anaesthetic gas while he extracted five of my teeth.

My mouth started to regain some feeling as I came round washing and spitting the blood into the bowl. Mam held my hand and comforted me as well as she could stroking my forehead. She knew I had been through an ordeal. I was pleased to leave the torture chamber and return to the fresh air and warm sunshine.

"How about an ice lolly?" William "I think it will soothe your gums."

I answered in the affirmative with my rubbery floppy lips doing their best to mumble a thank you. A multicoloured rocket lolly lubricated my parched and tender mouth and we had fruit jelly and pink blancmange for tea.

At school the next day I was the subject of intense interrogation about my experience. I was quite proud to proclaim the number of fillings and extractions I had endured. "Gas or needle?" Was the question most asked meaning local or general anaesthetic "Oh I had both!" describing my face being swallowed by the mask. "Did it hurt?"

I had the option here to say it was excruciating but in reality it was more uncomfortable and scary than painful. However my gums were very sore. So I could seek sympathy for the pain I had suffered or lie through my remaining teeth what a brave little soldier I had been. For the rest of my life I did my best to avoid the dentist until methods and equipment had improved dramatically and was most fortunate to find a close friend who was a dentist.

In that era it was common practice for children to have their tonsils removed, a surgical operation to remove fleshy pads at the back of the throat. Tonsilitis was a viral infection causing the pads to swell and painful like a sore throat. Regular infections resulted in an overnight stay in hospital, general anaesthetic, toast and jelly and ice cream. I remember my stay on the children's ward feeling very lonely and isolated. Mam and Dad had taken me in, telling me to be brave, it would soon be over and back home tomorrow. I had the operation i the afternoon along with five other terrified kids all lined up on a trolley , like a fairground ride, and conveyed to the theatre. We waited in a side room until, one by one, we were taken in to the operation theatre. I came round back on the ward with a bowl to spit out the blood and gooey residue of the anaesthetic. We were left to whimper and shout for our Mam's or the nurse but we were on our own. There was no better sight than Mam striding down the ward to take me home. She often said that it improved my health and I was a far stronger child thereafter.

Mam was a good provider making the most of everything. She tailored most of her own clothes using patterns from Woman's Realm magazine; second-hand jumpers from a church jumble sale would be unravelled and re-knitted into jumpers and balaclavas. I was her winding rack, sitting on a chair with both arms outstretched and my thumbs up so that she could wind the loops of wool from hand to hand and then twist them into a ball ready for re-knitting.

Balaclava wearing was virtually compulsory for every child. It is a strange name but came from a village in the Crimea War where British troops were freezing. In those days, we had four proper seasons: Spring, Summer, Autumn and Winter and no central heating. In winter, I often got out of bed with ice on the inside of the window! Freezing weather and snow lasted for weeks so a good balaclava was essential to keep warm and prevent earache. They were good for wiping away candles, two thick lines of clear, yellow or even green snot descending from both nostrils to the top lip. If not wiped or licked away they became encrusted in the neck of your balaclava. The great thing about balaclavas was you could roll the neck up so that it looked like a Commando soldier's cap comforter and then roll it down when on "Special Operations". We didn't need to black our faces as they were often grimy enough.

Another vital piece of warm clothing was a pair of hand knitted mittens joined with a long string of wool threaded up the arm of your heavy woollen overcoat, across the back and down the other arm so they never got lost. The back of a mitten was also useful for extinguishing the candles.

MY GANG

I didn't have a gang or belong to one because there was only me and Archibald Armour a lad the same age as me. We got on like a house on fire and were soon great friends. That is him on the left of the front cover. The building site was in several compounds, at the entrance was a vehicle yard fenced off with steel re-enforcement mesh panels for concrete, topped with razor wire left over from wartime defences. Double gates opened onto the street. Site vehicles were kept here together with cars owned by blokes who lived on the site and it was a parking spot for workers who lived off site.

Next to it, was our plot with several wooden dormitory cabins with beds for male workers. They had a stove, cooking facilities, an outside chemical toilet and washroom. Very basic but most blokes went home each weekend. Those in married quarters had a tin tent or mobile home with a toilet and hipbath, two bedrooms and a gas fire. Next to that was Mr. Simpkins' larger, more luxurious pre-fab at the side of the office cabin and all fenced off from the rest of us.

Archy and me

Then there was the building site, once a bombsite perhaps, obsolete Victorian brick factories or the remains of derelict terraced back-to-back insanitary houses. When the workers had gone home all this was our playground, our territory and we roamed every inch of it in search of adventure. We became expert climbers shimmying up pipes and scaffold poles, running along the wooden pathways in the sky and creating our own secret places. There was not much health and safety for the workers which was left to their own common sense, no plastic helmets just a cloth cap for protection. We were just told to be careful and don't get into trouble.

Everywhere was littered with bits of treasure for two young lads, timber, metal rods, screws and nails, roof tiles etc. Any worker dropping a nail would not stoop to pick it up even if he was at ground level. So Archy and me would gather all the dropped screws and nails, noggins of wood and anything that might come in handy. I would search the building site for every scrap of waste timber for the fire-pit Dad built outside the caravan. It was a good place to sit outside in the evenings Mam with knitting and Dad with his paper and me with a book or just staring into the flames and imagining what the future had in store.

Families with babies or young children got free National Dried Milk in tins large enough to make up seven pints of milk. They would go the Council House [Town Hall] to collect their milk and concentrated Welfare Orange Juice, thick, sweet and sickly neat from the bottle. Some mothers dipped the baby's dummy in it to stop them crying.I used to avoid calling for Archy early morning to avoid a compulsory dose of Scott's Emulsion containing cod liver oil.

The milk tins made great storage for our collections of nails that we meticulously sorted into four and six-inch round wire nails and different sizes of oval nails and we labelled each tin accordingly.

Being on our own we made our own entertainment chasing each other around the site in a game of tag, crossing gaps in daredevil fashion across a single plank, arms outstretched like tightrope walkers, or swinging hand over hand suspended from a scaffold pole. We became most agile like mountain goats or chimpanzees.

Play was not without some accidents though. In one chase I stood on a nail in a plank that went right through the sole of my wellington into the arch of my foot. I could not extract my foot nor lift the plank so I was marooned. Archy came to my aid standing on the plank either side of my foot. Holding the welly with both hands I pulled until the nail released its grip. I decided to keep my welly on until I got home where mother remonstrated and loved in equal measure, gently extracting my foot to reveal a bloody sock. There was a neat hole in my arch which she bathed with warm salt water, dried it and applied Germolene and a small fabric plaster. Germolene in a round tin, was a cure all, pink antiseptic cream scented with oil of wintergreen.

On another occasion, I fell and got something in my knee just below the kneecap. Just a scratch at first but in a matter of days it had ballooned into a large festering boil with a yellow head throbbing and threatening to erupt like a volcano. It needed more than Germolene so Dad took me to the local accident department at the hospital. A Sister in a blue uniform had a quick look and returned with some instruments of torture, a scalpel and a hot copper rod! Looking me squarely in the eyes she said,
"Be brave young man! Please hold his hands!"

Dad leaned over me placing a hand on each of mine, pinning them to the wooden bench. It all sounds much worse than it was but at the time it was terrifying as the scalpel lanced the top of the volcano and Sister heated the copper rod on a naked flame before inserting into the crater to poke out the yellow matter relieving the pressure. I thought that was it but next came a Kaolin poultice, a fine white clay used for making china pots, heated in its tin in a pan of water and spooned onto a gauze pad. Sister's eyes fixed mine again and I felt the pressure return from Dad's hands. "A little warm" she said as it was slapped on my knee, followed by a bandage. I was a brave little soldier, but the poultice had to be re-applied several times daily until all the pus had been drawn out.

My other knee was crowned with a wart in the centre of my knee cap and resisted all attempts to evict it with a variety of potions. A great deal of advice was proffered by the junior doctors at school based on old wives tales. For example rub it with bacon and then bury it and as the bacon rots the wart will wither away. Sounded more like witchcraft than medical science. Another wise child said I had to get the roots out. One afternoon in school I rose from my seat and as I turned swiped my knee on the edge of the desk leg resulting in a stream of blood down my leg. Teacher was not very happy and ready to blame me for doing something wrong or being stupid. But, the wart had gone root and all if there was one. A clean white hankie was rolled up and tied round my knee and the wart was never seen again, although I did hope that it might relocate on the teacher's nose!

Our site scavenging was not restricted to nails. The blokes would bring bottles of beer and pop from the local shop then leave them lying around. The screw tops were made of thick black Vulcanite that squashed an orange rubber washer to seal the neck. These bottles were true gold as there was a refund when returned to the shop, only pennies but they all added up. When the workers were on site they were restricted from leaving so we would run errands for pop, a paper from the offie or a pie from the butchers. The licensee at the offie got to know us well and he would let us take tobacco and beer if we put it in a shopping bag. He would see us out the door checking the local bobby was not on his rounds. For such errands we expected to keep the change or get a few pence in return. All proceeds were stored in our milk tins but apart from a homemade Vimto lolly from the offie or a bag of sweets, we had little idea what we might spend it on.

We were becoming entrepreneurs and always seeking other enterprises. Fridays were good for a fish and chip run, Archy wrote the orders down and I took the money. We had to get it right and be quick about it to avoid delivery of cold chips. The chippie appreciated our trade and often gave us a bag of chips or a potato fritter, one or two slices from a large potato in batter. If it was chips we asked for fish bits, the scraps of cooked batter strained from the dripping.

The pie run was even easier. Again, Archy took the orders, I sorted the money and timed our run to collect the pies and be back for the meal break. It proved very popular and lucrative. We often got a free pie each if we were lucky and I took mine home to share with Mam.

There was a lot of wood and much of it was chucked in an oil drum incinerator to get rid of it. Dad would get some 8 by 2 inch [no metric in them days] plank ends and run them through a bench saw into 9 inch lengths. Then, sitting on a stool in front of a log he would chop them into one inch slices and then into one inch sticks. Just right for kindling, lighting the fire.

We had seen nets of sticks for sale at the hardware shop, which fermented another money-making project. The grocer had onion nets or sacks and we had wood so it was a match made in heaven. Our delivery truck was an old pram and we went door to door selling our wares. We were cheaper than the ironmongers so kept well away from his shop. We had a select group of customers but one man was a cheat. He took a sack and then said it was underweight and he would not pay the full whack chucked his pennies at us and slammed the door. A few weeks later, we were ready for another delivery run. In our last sack, we hid a "half docker", half a building brick and knocked on his door. This time I held onto the sack while he weighed it and gave us the full amount. We didn't darken his door again.

From our vantage point in the crow's nest on top of the building, we often saw other kids playing in the street far below. Quite often, they would put their noses through the fence to see what was what. The whole site was our playground, our territory, but in a way it was also a prison as we occupied it on our own. I often thought that before demolition the site may have been their homes or factory and was certainly their playground, their territory. Now they were confined to the street and never allowed on site under any circumstances but that did not stop one or two trying to climb in. They were often thwarted by the wobbly fence topped with barbed wire. Archy and I were not allowed to play in the street but we could go to the shops across the road to run errands and we obviously encountered the locals. They were not a gang, just a bunch of kids playing street games and going to each other's houses. We were neither friends nor enemies. I think they understood the rules and we often talked through the fence. We were also useful as a valuable source of materials which we had in abundance: timber, nails, staples, metal rod, rope, in fact everything needed to make a trolley or go-cart, apart from the wheels, so we were happy to supply their needs. On one occasion, we swapped materials for a set of pram wheels and Archy and I made our own. We ran our little legs off towing each other round a makeshift circuit and even made ramps and bridges. Later we nailed a crate on the seat and used it to deliver kindling and empty bottles and collect pies.

Occasionally we did escape from our compound unseen. The site itself was vast and bordered the main street into town all down one side. If they needed to get the digger on site they would remove a panel so it could be driven in off the street. This was our chance to leg it towards town. On the corner stood an old style car garage repairing cars and selling Esso petrol and it was always our first call pleading for "Esso" badges. I cannot recall the attraction or fascination but it was just good to get a badge and you can just make it out on my hand-knitted pullover on the front cover. Round the corner was a sweet shop run by Mrs Bridges who made Vimto ice-lollies for one penny! In the 60s and 70s we enjoyed a "Thrupenny Jubbly" a frozen orange drink in a strange-shaped wax carton. Unless you had scissors or a knife, they were difficult to get into so you could suck the juice and quench your thirst. You were left with a large block of ice to play with and occasionally and mischievously drop it down someone's neck.

On our way back we would go past a small factory where they bottled drinks, pop and beer so we always had a look to see what was going on. On one such visit we came across their delivery truck parked on the access road off the main street. We had great fun running and jumping on to the back until it started to slowly roll forward, gathering speed down the incline, crossed the main street and came to a halt against the church wall opposite. Time for a quick exit!

FUN AND GAMES

Mostly, Archy and I made our own entertainment. There was no telly, just the radio, but in those days it was exciting to hear stories of derring do like Biggles Special Air Police.

Mam and Dad always had a lot to do but sometimes we would sit round the table and play cards, gambling with match sticks. Newmarket was based on horseracing and from a second deck of cards you took out Jack, Queen, King and Ace from different suites and these were put on the table to be the horses in the race. You placed bets by putting sticks on the horse of your choice and if you could play any of the matching horses, you picked up the winnings. I played Brag with Dad a lot and tried to restrain my excitement at a good hand, keep a straight face or poker face as he called it. If I was on my own I would play patience or solitaire just with a pack of cards as there were no computers or tablets then.

Occasionally, on a Sunday, Archy and his parents would call in for the evening and we would play Tip It. All you need is a tanner [sixpenny piece] and a group sitting round a table. We passed the coin from hand to hand under the table and then placed closed fists on the tabletop. One person had to guess where it stopped and tell the person to "Tip It." Sometimes you could tell from the whites of a player's knuckles if they had the hidden tanner. Good clean simple fun especially if played with a poker face.

One Christmas I received a Monopoly board game from my grandparents. The players went round the board by throwing a dice and the aim was buy as much of the property as possible, places we had only heard of like, Mayfair, Old Kent Road and

Marylebone Station. You could buy houses and hotels to put on your property so any player landing on them had to pay you a rent. At the end of the game, the one with the most money was the winner but, we hardly ever finished a game because it took so long and the table had to be cleared for tea or breakfast.

Another Christmas or birthday Mam and Dad bought me a Meccano set containing reusable pre-drilled metal strips, plates, angle girders, wheels, axles and gears, that you bolted together to make working models and mechanical devices. Of course, me Dad was a great help explaining how to build bridges and other things he had not blown up as a Sapper.

Red and white. Blue and white. Claret and blue. Yellow. Black and white and many other combinations would pass though the nearby streets on the way to the football ground nearby. In those days, they were all pretty well behaved, not too noisy and the pie shop and chippy would do a good trade feeding the away supporters. The pubs did well too sometimes spilling out on to the pavement. With Dad being a scouser, he could only support one of two clubs, "The Toffees" Everton or Liverpool. When I was old enough he took me to watch Liverpool standing on the famous Kop. I will never forget the first time we sang "You'll never walk alone." as loudly and passionately as I could with the hairs standing up on the back of my neck with excitement. Then the roar as the boys in red emerged onto the pitch. I was now a confirmed Liverpool fan. The name of the Kop comes from a famous battle for a hill called Spion Kop in the Boer War where many soldiers from Lancashire were killed.

Archy would come round most Saturday mornings and listen to Uncle Mac on the BBC Light programme, before Radio One and Two came along. Originally, his programme was called Children's Choice and then Children's Favourites where kids could write in asking for requests. Bang on ten past nine, Uncle Mac always started with, "Hello children, everywhere!"

But the bestest was when Mam went to town shopping or getting her hair permed and she took us to the local "flea pit", the flicks or cinema for children's film club. There was always a long queue of over-excited kids like us ready to pay a tanner [2.5p] for a morning of adventure and escapism. When the doors opened the flood of kids charged in trying to get the best seats in the middle of the back rows.

It was a complete show with Mickey Mouse cartoons and, ongoing serials with the Lone Ranger or Flash Gordon. The film would always finish with the hero about to come to a nasty end and you had to come back the following week to see how the hero escaped, but of course, we would often miss the next episode.

Shows usually started with a singsong generated by a compere, then games like eating a doughnut on a string the fastest or a singing contest where a huge glitzy organ, a Wurlitzer, rose out of the orchestra pit to play sing along songs. Just like karaoke, the words were written on the screen and a white ball bounced from word to word in time to the tune.

The main feature was Flash Gordon or Zorro but my favourite was a typical cowboys and gunslingers western. There was a constant noise from the packed audience until it came to the final showdown between the Sherriff and "Quick Draw" McGraw the villainous gunslinger with more than twenty notches on his Colt revolver. Sherriff and outlaw stared each other out on the main street in the hot sun, sweat trickling down their brows, trigger fingers twitching ready to draw. Now there was silence, as we sat on the edge of our seats in suspense, followed by rapturous cheers as the gunslinger fell face down in the dirt.

The best though, were the chases on horseback, the Sherriff's posse pursuing the outlaws who had just robbed the bank. This was the time to join them by leaping astride the seat in front, slapping your left thigh to make the seat gallop faster and then shooting the baddies with the "index finger revolver" that never needed reloading. The attendants took a dim view of this activity but it was almost impossible to control, especially if you were the cavalry riding to the rescue of the encircled wagon train under Indian attack. One lad next to me was defending the wagons and shooting the Indians riding round and round, and then suddenly he would squeal and collapse back on his seat clutching an imaginary arrow in his chest. Seconds later, he had fully recovered to continue firing.

Zorro was a masked righter of wrongs armed only with his sword that he wielded with expert precision. Back at the site, Archy and I became Zorro with our navy blue school raincoats over our shoulders and buttoned at the neck like Zorro's cloak. We cut masks from Cornflake packets and galloped around the site on imaginary horses, brandishing homemade swords tipped with chalk. On Monday morning, builders were asking questions about who had been leaving Zorro's calling card of a Z.

HOLIDAYS

My earliest recollection of going on holiday was a bed and breakfast or boarding house at Barwick Street in the side streets of Scarborough, just inland from the Grand Hotel on the far side of the town centre. It was a very ordinary street of mainly long brick terraces with little walled front gardens.

We set off early Saturday morning for the steam train and took nearly all day having to change at various stations. I loved sticking my head out of the window to smell the steam and the smoke from the engine but got a tongue-lashing from Mam for getting all smutty. Dragging me back down to my seat, she licked her fresh white hanky and scrubbed my face clean. For me it was a great adventure with frequent visits to the buffet car and observing all the passengers, mainly bound for the seaside. It was my first real glimpse of the world outside of the building site, industrial buildings and smoking chimneys giving way to suburbia, the fields and rivers of the countryside and then the historical city of York and the Minster. The station was once the largest in the world with thirteen platforms, and cavernous, curving, arched roofs and we stopped briefly at platform four to pick up more holidaymakers then on to the seaside.

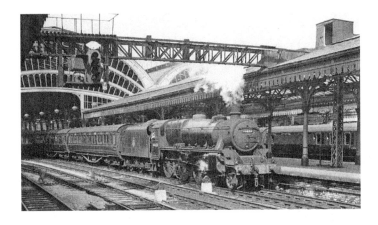

London Midland Train at York Station

We didn't have money for a taxi so walked to our lodgings run by our landlady Mrs. Edith Cuthbert. I found her quite frightening at first, as she had a withered leg and a built up shoe so she limped and clomped as she walked. Mam later explained the lady had polio as a child and she was now a war-widow taking in lodgers for a living. We got a warmish reception, cup of tea and a biscuit as she explained the rules of the household. In by 10pm out by 10am. Breakfast sharp at 8am, dinner at 5pm. Leave the shared bathroom clean and tidy and flush the toilet. Buy your own toilet paper.

Pots of tea and milky drinks were extra. Dinner was an odd affair because Mrs. Cuthbert would only cook what Mam bought that day! So on our first day we missed dinner and went out for fish and chips. Mam was not too chuffed at going shopping on her holiday and vowed not to go there again. Compared to some B&Bs this was a luxury as some had an electric hotplate in the bedroom to cook your own meals including breakfast.

Liz outside Barwick Street

The Dakin Famly outside Barwick Street lodgings

Architecturally, Dad and me were surprised at the style and variation of brickwork. On the right side of the street, the bricks were pale anaemic grey but the opposite side was built with orangey red bricks laid in a chequer-board style with alternating yellowy bricks. Most odd, but they added a little brightness and colour to an otherwise drab area. Dad and I discussed how difficult it would have been for the brickies to get all the bricks in the right order. The roof pitch was also quite shallow with roof lights so there must have been a third floor in the loft.

I think there were three bedrooms on the second floor. I guess Mrs. Cuthbert had the little box room. Ours was at the front with a double bed and my cot or camp bed. Flowery patterned wallpaper and yellowing white gloss did little to brighten the room shaded by net curtains and lit by a single low wattage bulb under a pink lampshade. Two bedside units and matching chest of drawers were all "Utility" furniture, basic brown varnish made from cheap timber and plywood, being the only items available post war. Our beds had clean white sheets, heavy woollen blankets and a candlewick bedspread.

Sunday morning Dad was up first to use the communal bathroom and then he and I set off down the promenade to a newspaper shop on the sea front for his daily paper and tobacco. Just like when he used to call at Mam's offie. He sat on a bench reading and enjoying his first cigarette of the day whilst I examined the flotsam and jetsam on the tide line and picked up a few shells.

We were back just in time for breakfast, Mam was at the table waiting for us talking to a lady on the next table. They seemed to be getting on very well and it turned out they were from Derbyshire as well, a little town called Ashbourne. Her name was Mrs. Dakin and she was there for the week with her husband Sydney and daughter Elizabeth, about my age. Elizabeth, holding her Teddy Edward to her chest, managed a smile in my direction.

Breakfast was basic, but substantial if you liked what was on offer. There was no choice. Cornflakes, Bacon and egg, sliced white toast, Mother's Pride I think, and jam. Pot of tea. Glass of milk for the boy. On Sundays, you got a sausage as well. If you wanted an extra pot of tea anytime or a hot milky drink before bed these were all extras so some evenings we walked down the prom to a cafe where they served Horlicks using a machine that whipped it into a froth. I had Ovaltine and Dad a pot of builder's.

"Fred. Better go to the toilet before we go out for the day."
Ablutions completed we set off for the beach with costume rolled up in a towel. I had proper swimming trunks not like the ones that mams and grandmas knitted out of wool. As soon as they got wet, they were all soggy and started to fall down. A stop en route to buy a bucket and red metal spade and we secured our little patch of sand with two hired deck chairs. Dad wore his cap, collar and tie and sports jacket and Mam was in a long flowery dress and cardigan. Not quite her Sunday best.

Sydney and Hazel Dakin

Mother read one of her romantic paperback novels of lost loves while Dad read the paper and did the crossword. For them a holiday was clearly a complete break from the monotonous daily struggle and toil of work and keeping house. They needed a rest. All I wanted to do was dig holes, make sandcastles, fill ditches with seawater that soaked away, and bury my legs in the sand.

The Dakins turned up and occupied the patch of beach next us so Elizabeth and I played together digging and making sandcastles. It was good having Elizabeth to play ball with, paddle and splash in the sea or just sitting in a deck chair chatting. We went on the donkeys and also met at the fun fair on the roundabouts. At Peasholm Park we raced each other round the lake in small paddle boats and I won because my arms were a lot stronger.

CHARLIE PARKES

The Punch and Judy show came to the beach and I was allowed to take a few pennies and go and watch the show, under strict instructions not to wander off and stay at the show. I was intrigued and watched the performance several times but then realised that the show had changed location by some distance as it moved from the South Shore to the North Shore. I was now lost or rather I did not know where Mam and Dad were. I stayed put and, eventually, I saw me Dad, just like the cavalry, coming to my rescue and delivering a pretend clip on my ear, which I ducked as he put an arm round my shoulder. Mam gave me a bit of a tongue-lashing followed by a hug and we all had an ice cream.

One day Dad put down his paper on hearing the sound of a large powerful engine roaring away somewhere on the beach.
"That sounds like a DUKW." Said Dad.
Me and Mam looked at each other and Mam said "All I can hear are sea gulls."
"Not a bird duck! A D...U...K...W, a six-wheel-drive amphibious vehicle like we had on D-Day."

Sure enough, the strange creature roared along the beach and stopped at a little booth where a couple of men in Army uniform were selling tickets for a ride to the sea and back. Dad was off like a shot with mother declining and preferring her steamy novel. I had no choice as Dad grabbed my hand and we ran to the DUKW. Dad spent some time reminiscing with the guys in uniform before we climbed a ladder and took our seats.

Amphibious Vehicle DUKW

He was so excited recounting his exploits to me and explaining how the DUKW was able to go on land and sea. It was clear that it had taken him back to his days as a Sapper heading for the Normandy beaches, reliving every moment and then wiping a few tears with his white hanky.
"Are you Ok Dad?"
"Aye Fred just a bit of sand in my eye."

I recall that each November he had "sand in his eye" at the Remembrance Day Parade in the town. Recovering his demob suit from the wardrobe, he pressed it to military uniform standards. Boots highly polished, regimental tie and a crisp white shirt, a red poppy in his lapel, his medals worn proudly on his chest and his Army beret he was ready for the parade. Mam and I watched as he joined all the ex-servicemen marching to a band down to the town war memorial. After the last post sounded on the bugle, he spent time with his colleagues, shaking hands, patting backs and swopping the latest gossip. Then we were off to the Royal British

Legion for beer, sandwiches and cake. Mam and I left Dad to reminisce with his mates.

Sunday had been quite busy with loads of day-trippers, so Monday was a lot quieter. After our compulsory sojourn to the beach, I was given a wiping down and we walked along the bay-front shops and arcades. I was eager to try my luck in the arcades with a bag of pennies I had withdrawn from my powdered milk tin. We spent an entertaining hour losing and winning but eventually my last penny was teetering on the edge of the push the penny game. If only I had one more penny to push it over the edge with a lot more coppers. I then heard Mr Clelland's wise words echoing in my brain,
"Look after the pennies and the pounds will look after themselves."
Well I did have some fun playing on the machines but now my pennies were gone and I could have done something better with

them.

There were plenty of other attractions to take my mind off my losses. Crabbing in the harbour with a bit of bacon rind smuggled from the breakfast table, Scarborough Castle and going walks round the bays. Mother wanted to look round the shops and buy saucy post cards, so we found Boyes three-storey department store on the corner of Queen Street. I had never seen so many different things for sale in one place. In fact, I never knew that half of them existed. We started at the top and mother disappeared into the ladies department while Dad and I made it to the toy department. It was like Father Christmas's warehouse with every toy, book and game imaginable, mostly too expensive for my holiday pocket money. However, I came across a blue and silver embossed tin with a hinged lid bearing the title Oxford set of Mathematical Instruments complete and accurate with a picture of a building that looked like an Oxford College. The tin contained a metal self-centring compass, a small pencil, pencil sharpener, eraser, 6" ruler, 45° & 60° set squares, 180° protractor, a lettering stencil and a timetable with a maths fact sheet on the back.

"Just right for doing your joiner's rods Fred." Dad enthused.
"Why not get that and a drawing pad and pencil set? There's room in the tin for the pencils." Dad was right and persuasive but spending my holiday money meant less to spend on ice cream. He could see I was troubled and offered half towards it.

BOY FROM THE BUILDING SITE

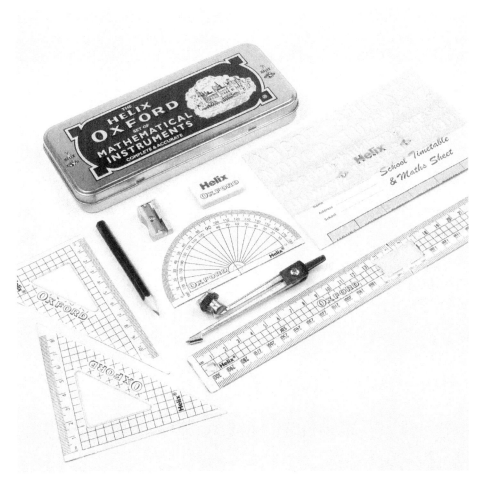

I took my items to the cash desk where a nice lady dressed like Miss Primly smiled warmly as I counted out my shillings. She pressed the keys on the large ornate cash register and I saw the price pop up in the window, a bell rang and a receipt shot out of a slot, which she popped into a brown paper carrier bag with my set.

The holiday was not all about entertaining me because it was a week free from the toils, trials and tribulations of work for Mam and Dad. They needed the time to rest, relax and recuperate ready for another year of hard labour. Their treat was a morning walk along the promenade to the Suncourt Enclosure where they could lie back in deck chairs and listen to Max Jaffa a famous violinist and bandleader of the Palm Court Orchestra. Mam and I listened to him on the radio but it was fantastic to hear and see him play live.

Suncourt Enclosure Scarborough

My favourite and bestest day was the visit to Peasholm Park. Mam loved the beds of colourful flowers and the acres of neatly trimmed lawns where we could play or just sit and watch the world go by or have a picnic. All she had at home was sand, dust and rubble and a few dandelions. Dad and I went in a rowing boat on a large lake with rocks and cliffs like a mountain on one side and an amphitheatre-style grandstand on the other. In front of the seating was a bandstand in the lake with a walkway to the shore and about 3pm onwards people flocked to get a seat ready for the show.

The posters said it was the "Battle of Peasholm" a naval battle on the lake. A man stood in the bandstand and over the microphone got us to boo and hiss at the enemy and cheer for our ships as 20-foot replica ships and a submarine fired shots at each other. Pretend shells splashed in the water next to the ships and there was a lot of noise and smoke. Then he got us to cheer for the RAF as two jet planes on wires screamed over us and out over the lake bombing the baddies. Of course, the good guys won after thirty minutes and then the tops of the boats lifted off to reveal a person in each boat taking the applause for their performance. That was really good.

Battle of Peaseholm

Nearly as good was a trip to Treasure Island on the Hispaniola. It looked like a proper pirate ship and I had seen pictures in Robert Louis Stevenson's book. I met Elizabeth and her parents there and we sailed along The Mere to the island where staff dressed as pirates escorted us to 'Treasure Island'. The treasure was imitation gold coins hidden in the sandy soil and we grabbed wooden branches and sticks to search for the hidden treasure. I remember frantically swiping at the soil with a tree branch, anxious to find a doubloon, which I did and got a certificate but those who didn't find one got the dreaded black spot.

Hispaniola

The pirates were very convincing being both fearsome and friendly, especially Long John Silver with one leg and a crutch who was talking with Mr Dakin. Turns out, they knew each other from the war where Long John lost his leg. He had buried some coins and pointed to a spot with his crutch whispering to Elizabeth, "Dig there young lady".

The days flew by and Saturday morning came all too soon as we said goodbye to the Dakins and my new friend Elizabeth. Mrs Dakin, Hazel to her friends, had captured our happy holiday moments on her Kodak Brownie 127 camera and promised to send some snaps.

The return journey was something of an anticlimax without the excitement of going on holiday. At least I could look forward to telling Archy all about my travels and adventures, meeting Elizabeth and, hopefully, show him some pictures as well.

"I'll put the kettle on!" said Mam as soon as we got in, plonking a bag of shopping on the table that we picked up on the way back from the station.

"I'll just check everything is in order outside." said Dad, going for a wander around the vans and a quick roll-up.

I went to my room and took out a small wooden crate from the top of my wardrobe. It was my treasure chest where I kept my collection of interesting bits and pieces, shells, driftwood and my Treasure Island certificate, and Elizabeth's address, all now preserved and ready to invoke memories of happy times.

WALTERS AND ARMOUR - PRIVATE INVESTIGATORS

I think Mr. Simpkins was a bully as no one liked him very much and he always seemed to be ranting and telling the builders off. I think he felt he was above everyone else and full of his own self-importance. He wore a dark suit and stout boots and if he went on site he would roll his trouser bottoms up to keep them clean. His round wire-framed NHS prescription glasses sat on his nose above a pencil line moustache. Always a shirt and tie and his hair slicked down with Brilliantine and parted down the middle. Today his hair would be a skin fade but there were no such hair-dos in those days. It was short back and sides at the barbers or your Mam did it with a pudding bowl on your head trimming round the edge. Luckily Dad had an ex Army friend who was a barber so we would visit him for tea and fruit cake. His wife did my hair finishing it off with a pink creamy setting lotion combed in tramlines before it set into ridges like a ploughed field. It felt awful, all hard and crispy and I couldn't wait to get home and wash it off.

Any road up, Mr. Simpkins seldom ventured on the site as his presence often resorted in a hammer or handful of nails clattering down the scaffolding in his direction.

"Sorry Mr. Simpkins. Didn't see you there." Someone else would shout, "better luck next time!" as he scurried away.

He always wore a bowler hat, probably for protection and possibly as a symbol of his position. Anyone going for a job was advised to knock and wait to be called in and on entering, remove his cap in deference to Mr. Simpkins. There was a tale of one chap who kept his cap on much to Mr. Simpkins' annoyance, and told him that he should remove it when in his office.

"I've come here for a bloody job not a haircut!"

There was a time when Mr. Simpkins was complaining to the men about them using too many materials, too much wastage and materials going missing.

"Mark my words I have got my eyes peeled for anyone stealing off the site."

That created quite an atmosphere with the workers feeling they were under suspicion. A few weeks later two men arrived on site and had a long talk with Mr. Simpkins. Turned out they were security from head office. A smart looking couple of blokes, in suits with trilbies, who toured the site talking to the men. I guess they were ex-coppers, CID probably. They were not making accusations or putting the frighteners on them, just asking questions about site management, stock control, security and so on. Oh, and had they seen anything suspicious. They gave out cards with contact numbers for the men to call if they had any information.

Saturday evening Mam and Dad would often go to the local pub with the Armours leaving me and Archy to our own devices, and I don't mean Ipads, Iphones or gaming tablets. I mean entertain ourselves with cards, jigsaws or roaming the site. It was late in the autumn, the evenings were quite dark, and there was little or no light on the site, just a glow from the occupied caravans. All the single workers went home for the weekend or were chasing a bit of skirt round the town. About 7.30 Archy and I left the caravan, switched the lights off and wandered round the site. It was an industrial building and by now reached several stories so we would climb to our crow's nest and look out over a dark sea sprinkled with lights from the town. A pick-up came along the street and stopped at the gate to Mr. Simpkin's compound and the storage units. The gate opened to reveal the unmistakeable outline of a rotund little man with short legs wearing a bowler hat. It was Mr. Simpkins. He had a long hard look towards the cabins all in darkness and, opening both gates waved the truck in and quickly shutting the gates. The truck seemed familiar but it was difficult to see any detail in the dark apart from a broom and a box on a pole fixed to the rack behind the cab.

Mr. Simpkins opened the doors to the store sheds and he and the driver started loading up 8x2s [8 by 2 inch planks or rafters], rolls of roofing felt, a long wooden ladder and a couple of scaffold boards. These were too long for the truck floor but it had a rack behind the cab to rest them on. Then, the hardware store for small sacks of nails. The driver earned a stiff expletive ridden rebuke for creating a noise when throwing the bags on the truck. The paint store was next and out came gallon tins of gloss and undercoat and emulsion. Finally, they loaded several bags of cement before hurriedly closing everything up and exiting through the gate. Archy and I watched open-mouthed not believing what we had seen. We knew it was Simpkins by his shape, the bowler hat and all the keys for the stores. We could not make out the other man but the truck looked familiar. We were sure we had seen it in the site car park then Archy remembered the hod carrier who worked for the brickies. He had a hod carrier, a box on a pole for holding bricks. We always admired his strength up and down ladders all day with such a load on his shoulder. He had a pick-up and it was not in the car park.

W&A Private Investigators made their way quietly back to their caravan climbing in through the back window and slipping under the bed covers where, after a lot of excited chatter and speculation they fell asleep. The Armours must have carried Archy off to their van because I was alone in the morning. We had discussed what we should do but now it was down to me. After a quick flannel wash I appeared at the breakfast table.

"All quiet last night then Will?" enquired Dad.

Did he know something or was it just a check to see that all was well? I had a mouth full of toast so could only mumble an incoherent reply. Mam joined in,

"What did you two get up to? No mischief I hope."

"We went up to the crow's nest to look at the town and ...."

I told them exactly what we had seen. Dad checked the details over and over to make sure he understood everything and that I had not forgotten anything or been mistaken.

"Well Sherlock Holmes you and Dr. Watson you had a most exciting evening. Now I don't want you to say anything to anyone. Understand? You both did really well. Now leave this to me".

Dad finished his mug of builder's before disappearing with a pocketful of penny coins. When he returned there was a long quiet discussion with Mam.

Monday morning Dad was away from the breakfast table bright and early. Mr. Simpkins was at the clocking on point checking who was in, who was late and dishing out instructions for the day's work. All seemed quite normal and Dad went to his job on the site. Mr. Simpkins went back to his office. About 8.30 a black car pulled into the compound, which was rather odd as only Mr. Simpkins and delivery vehicles were allowed in. Out stepped the two men in trilbies who marched swiftly into his office without knocking or waiting to be invited in. There seemed to be some shouting and gesticulating until the hod carrier's truck reversed in driven by the hod carrier. Sitting in the passenger seats were two more trilbies. All the stolen materials were still on the truck, but even though the game was up, Simpkins tried to blame the hod carrier and congratulated the trilbies for catching him. The trilbies had a quiet word with Simpkins explaining that he could admit his part and get the sack or it was a trip to the police station. He was dumbstruck.

The two thieves were set to work returning all the stolen materials to the stores to a chorus of cheers from the building site. Simpkins was marched round to his pre-fab to clear his belongings, raising even louder cheers from the workers as he and the hod carrier began loading his possessions onto the hod carrier's truck. Mrs. Simpkins was voicing her objections in no uncertain and rather unpleasant terms at the top of her shrill voice and telling her husband what she thought of him. Eventually she appeared at the door carrying two suitcases, her handbag looped over her wrist. Spitting a string of venomous expletives at anyone and everyone, she strutted to their car throwing her suitcases unceremoniously in the back and slamming her passenger door behind her.

It was a great show for the workforce waiting to see the grand finale and the final curtain for Mr. Simpkins. Appearing at the door, he was subjected to a spontaneous clanging of tools on the scaffolding and shouts of

"Take yer caps off lads!"

Simpkins straightened his tie and bowler and tried to leave with what little dignity he had left.

As he drove out, a Jaguar saloon in British Racing Green pulled into the compound and out stepped the boss, Mr. Clelland and his personal assistant Miss Joanna Primly. By this time, Archy

and I were in the pound seats on the scaffold watching the goings on. Mr. Clelland surveyed his jubilant workforce,

"Ok chaps. Show's over!"

Almost to a man, the workers touched the peaks of their cloth caps in salute and respect before returning to their labours.

One brave soul managed a wolf whistle but Miss Primly's glare was enough to silence him. The workers made various comments, some unrepeatable and should not have reached the ears of such tender young boys, but we did not fully understand what they meant anyway.

"Is that his knocking piece?"
"Is she his bit on the side or his bit of stuff?"
I suppose they meant his girlfriend.

Whatever she was, she certainly looked the business in a black pencil line slim-fitting skirt to just below the knee and a white blouse with a frilled collar and puffed sleeves. I recognised her outfit from Mam's magazines and I also noticed the effect of her Playtex lift and separate bra that appeared regularly in the appropriately named Tit Bits. A wide black patent belt, matching her stiletto shoes, emphasised her narrow waist. Her long dark hair beautifully styled in an elegant beehive accentuated her high cheekbones. Black-framed spectacles hung around her neck on a chain framing her narrow face, her lips adorned in bright red lipstick.

The workers looked on in awe.
"Bet she's wearing sussies!" whispered one longingly.
I knew that sussies were suspenders because Mam wore them but she always hung them up to dry in the caravan, out of public view with her stockings and smalls. There must have been something about them that caused greater excitement as one grew up.

Miss Primly followed Mr. Clelland into the office and with the show now over, the workers returned to their tasks speculating on what had been going on.
"Fancy that cheeky bastard Simpkins trying to blame us for shortages and waste."
They didn't have long to wait for more information. At tea break the workers gathered outside the office and Mr. Clelland, accompanied by Miss Primly, addressed them, explaining that Simpkins and his brother-in-law, the hod carrier, had been caught bang to rights and had been detained by the trilbies, his security staff.

After the tea break, Dad was about to return to his job when Miss Primly asked him to step into the office. This caused another round of chatter and interest. Dad was taken aback but not too surprised.

"Jimmy come on in and take a seat" said Mr. Clelland, rising from his chair and offering his hand.

"I cannot thank you enough for your actions because we have been after the blighter for some time. You have saved the firm a fortune and it is never pleasant being under suspicion and having to work with rogues and thieves."

Dad nodded.

"We have the boys Will and Archy to thank. They saw what was going off and had the courage to tell me what was what."

"I will speak to them later and thank them but first we need to sort out a new site manager." responded Mr. Clelland as Miss Primly passed him a file.

"Thank you Joa er Miss Primly. Now Jimmy you are a time served joiner with lots of experience, joined up as a Sapper, landed on D-Day so you experienced all manner of construction and deconstruction....."

"Aye I always said that in the war I built things and blew them up!"

"Well as you know my company does both. We demolish and build for a new Britain, good homes, clean efficient factories, bridges, roads and railways and water treatment plants. In fact we can build anything."

Dad nodded wondering where all this was leading.

"So Jimmy you have experience of leading and commanding men, you were a Lance Corporal, getting the job done in the most dangerous and difficult circumstances. You have worked on a lot sites, met a lot of men, you know all their trades and all their tricks and what's more you talk their language and command their respect. Jimmy I want you as my new site manager. Starting today, what do you say?"

Dad was flummoxed. Flabbergasted.

"Not like a Scouser to be short of words Mr. Clelland but I am truly surprised. Like you say I know the tricks of the trades but what about paperwork, hiring and firing and all that?"

"Joa, er Miss Primly will help you out and you will soon get the hang of it. She is a great organiser and has arranged for two ladies to clean the office. She will check that all the files are in order and the cleaners will give Simpkins' pre-fab a good firking out so that you, Vee and William can move in. What do you say?"

"I say yes Mr. Clelland. Definitely yes!"

At lunch break the speculation ended as Jimmy was introduced as the new manager to a rousing cheer and applause.
"First job then Jimmy is to go and tell Vee she is moving to bigger and better quarters then you had better start looking for a joiner to take your place."
They shook hands warmly.
"We had better see Archy and William now. Bring them to my office."

Jimmy rushed to tell Vee the news and she was delighted. After a quick wipe-down with a flannel, William and Archy went to see Mr Clelland who shook their hands and thanked them for keeping an eye on his site.
"It was such a brave thing to do and it was the right thing to do to tell Dad. Honesty is always the best policy you know. Good work deserves just reward." he said taking a large billfold wallet from his suit jacket and removing two £10 notes. Lost for words the boys managed to mumble a thank you to Mr. Clelland who advised,
"Now give this to your mothers and tell them to put it in your Post Office accounts and make good use of it. Remember the saying, "Look after the pennies and the pounds will look after themselves. Mam will tell you what that means."

Now Jimmy, I'll leave you in Joa er Miss Primly's capable hands. She will be staying at the Carlton Hotel for the rest of the week and will be in the office to show you how to go on, how we like things doing. See you on Friday."

With that, Mr. Clelland jumped in his Jaguar and left the site.

Dad started to get things organised with a lot of help and advice from Miss Primly. Vee loved the pre-fab, now all spick and span from "a good firkin out" by the cleaning ladies.

Bang on 2pm, Mr. Clelland arrived in his Jaguar to check all was well and whisked Joa er Miss Primly off "to view some other building projects" but only they knew what that actually meant.

On Friday's the workmen finished early for the weekend so when the siren sounded they all appeared at our old van and carried all our possessions to our new home. Mam hurried round trying to get everything in the right place, beds made, clothes hung up, food stored away, pots and pans in the kitchen drawers. Finally, about six o'clock she was satisfied and sat down to admire her new home.
"Come on Fred, I think it is fish supper tonight." Dad said as he put the kettle on to boil. "Back in a few minutes Vee."

On our return, the table was set, bread and butter, tomato ketchup, salt and vinegar, and best china!
"I thought we ought to celebrate." Said Vee.
"So did I," said Dad plonking their Mackeson and Guiness bottles on the table.

You notice that sometimes, Mam and Dad called me Fred. It became a regular nickname and I never really understood why but it stands for Fred Fanackapan and I don't think he was a real person, like Joe Bloggs. He was a character in a song by Gracie Fields in the 1930s so perhaps that was the origin and was a common term of endearment between mother and child. So Fred it was.

After that incident W&A Private Investigators paid great attention to site security and the comings and goings, especially in the evenings when all was quiet and dark. The moonlight would cast eerie shadows around the constructions making our hearts skip a beat if we thought there was movement of a shadowy figure. The best vantage point was our crow's nest in the tops of the buildings. From here, we could remain hidden but see everything going on around us and in the adjoining streets. Mostly nothing happened but we consoled ourselves that we must be doing a good job if no one was trying to get in. Occasionally somebody tried the gates or started to climb the fence so we always kept some chunks of brick as ammo to throw at the intruders who scarpered sharpish, having no idea where they were being bombarded from.

Late one Saturday evening Archy and I sat in our crow's nest overlooking the vehicle park and saw the gate open wide enough to let two people in, a man and woman. Holding each other up, they staggered, giggling noisily, to the back of the compound and both climbed into the cab of the company's Bedford lorry. From our high position, we could not see what was going on, so we slithered quietly down the scaffold and climbed stealthily on to the back of the truck. Seeing movement through the small window in the back of the cab, we crawled quietly to get a better view. We were not a lot wiser because for kids of our age the activity was outside our knowledge and experience. In the dark we could just make out the man sitting in the driver's seat and the young lady sitting on his lap with both hands on the steering wheel, and she was bouncing up and down. One or both of them were making a lot of groaning noises. We both had small chrome torches that Mam got us from Woolies [Woolworths] and I motioned to Archy by putting a finger on my lips to be quiet. He nodded. I pointed to our torches and then showed three fingers, and pointed to the cab then the window. Finally, a signal with a thumb raised on my clenched fist to scarper. Archy smiled and nodded. One. Two. Three. Our torches flashed on illuminating the cab to reveal a lot of bare skin, followed by screaming, shouting and swearing as we leapt off the truck and into our jungle of scaffold pipes, just like Tarzan swinging through the trees.

Safely back in the crow's nest we watched the antics below. The lady was first to exit pulling her mini skirt down, before stomping off towards the gate in her white high heels. Judging by her language, she was not very amused. The man almost fell out of the cab with his trousers round his ankles, stumbling after her shouting "Doreeen! Doreeeen! Come back".

After that success, we kept a close watch on the vehicle compound, as it was the most insecure part of the site. Again, from the Crow's nest we heard the gate creak open and close and saw a shadowy figure creeping between the vehicles. From the back of a pick-up he took a jerry can and some piping and disappeared down the side of another lorry. He was there some time but returned with the jerry can, which must have been full because it looked quite heavy, loaded it on to his truck, and covered it with a tarpaulin, before leaving the compound as he had entered. We decided not to chuck a brick at him as we may hit a truck and perhaps better not flash our lights as he was obviously up to no good. Better to tell Dad.

Dad was quite thoughtful.
"Mmmm! That answers a few questions about fuel consumption on the firm's trucks. Well done lads! Well done indeed! You did the right thing; now leave the rest to me."
Dad told us to stay off the site in the evenings until further notice. At first, we didn't know that Dad had sent for the men in trilbies who must have kept observations while hiding in the compound. Any road up, sure enough, about a week later they pounced on the thief but this time the trilbies had been swapped for black woollen beanie hats and dark blue overalls, just like Commandos on a secret mission.

We were allowed back on patrol and the postman delivered a large brown paper package tied with string addressed to Mr W Walters and Mr A Armour! On the top were two of the biggest Cadbury Dairy Milk chocolate bars we had ever seen and a letter from Mr. Clelland thanking us once again for our vigilance. I didn't know what vigilance meant and had to look it up in Mam's pocket dictionary. Underneath were two large brand new torches with rechargeable batteries "so we could see right across the site."

SCHOOL

By the time I went to school at the age of six I was fairly fluent in builder-ese in several languages, well accents really, and an expert in swearing and insulting in words I did not fully understand. I was most fluent in Liverpool slang inherited from father but without swear words and insults. Mam had a Derbyshire twang with a few odd terms thrown in like:

It's Coad (It's cold)
Stop your chuntering (Stop complaining, mumbling)
Claarts are trousers) and kecks underwear
Gerrert (I don't believe you)
Got a bag on (Moaning or moody - "eez gorra reet bag on!"
Harping on (nagging or talking about something for an unreasonable period of time)
It's a bit black o'er Bill's mother's (There'll be a massive downpour any minute) I never knew where Bill's mother lived but there must have been many Bills with many mothers.
Is sen (himself)
Kerfuffle (panicked over something)
Alright me oad! (Hello my friend)
Pack up (packed lunch)
Shin tin (Is thee Mam there? No she isn't in)
Snap (food)
Stop mitherin (stop worrying)
Taitered (Worn out)
Teggies (Teeth, usually children's)
That looks manky (mouldy food, scabby knee going septic, that sort of thing)

I was exposed to North and South Yorkshire and a strange variation from the Sheffield area because some Sheffielders' are famously known to use the sound of 'D', instead of the traditional pronunciation of 'th', so "Where's dar bin den dee?"

There was a smattering of Irish on the site with their lilting tones and, of course, those from the north east broadly categorised as Geordie.
Howay, man! Let's go or hurry up
Wey aye, man! Yes! ...
Canny. Good, nice, or pleasant. ...
Gannin yem. Going home. ...
Am clamming. I'm so hungry. ...
What ye uptee the neet? What are you doing tonight? ...
Giz a deek? Let me have a look.

Geordie was tricky but the most difficult to master was Glaswegian. They had a language of their own with many words and terms totally alien to the Queen's English I would hear on the radio where even Scottish newsreaders sounded very English.

"Yur wee bassa" was often directed at myself and I suppose in polite English it would mean "You cheeky monkey." As I grew in confidence and was far enough away to secure my escape I would shout, "Yur wee bassa yursel Pal!"

Whilst the language was rather strong it was mainly meant in good humour and in any case we needed each other. They wanted Archy and me to run their errands, pick up dropped tools and so on and we needed their pennies, so we all got on amicably.

I had great fun imitating and would often creep up on a worker having a crafty fag or a gander at his newspaper and shout at him in scouse to get back to work.

Mam played a great part in my early education by reading to me from books she borrowed from the library. They were simple illustrated "look-and-say" reading schemes used in primary schools. Mam would get me to say what I saw and then I memorised the words. As my reading improved, we moved on to Famous Five adventures. Mam had Tit Bits magazine and Woman's Realm so I would leaf through those looking at the pictures and adverts and try to pronounce words like "corselette". Mam would say,

"You don't need to know about things like that!" and underline or ring words from the headlines for me to copy.

I was pretty good at maths, counting pennies, and working out change at a time when there were 240 pennies to a pound, 12 to a shilling and 6 to a tanner and 3 to a thruppenny bit, crowns or five bob and half a crown, two and six. I could recite my times tables up to twelve and do multiplication and division. Mam knew how to grab and maintain my interest by using building examples,

"If Dad is cutting eight feet long rafters and needs 7 rafters how many feet of wood would he need." And "How many lengths could he cut from one piece of wood thirty two feet long?"

I also knew about weights from ounces to hundredweights and pints and gallons as all building materials like nails, paints and cement had their weight marked on the bags or tins. Not only that, but I knew all the types and shapes of nails, round and oval and the gauge or thickness. Not only that, I knew what they were used for as well. I knew angles so I suppose I was good at geometry. All Dad's work involved angles for cutting roof timbers and building frames so I used his T Square to draw right angles and roofer's triangle to mark up the required angle on the end of a rafter. Dad would bring site plans home to work on and so I would measure and copy them to scale.

I surprised my teachers with my drawing ability, not so much in an artistic way but a technical way. If the teachers said draw a house, most kids would draw a rectangle freehand, two square windows and a door. I used a ruler to get straight lines and create a three-dimensional perspective to scale.

I also knew feet and inches and helped to measure pieces of wood he was working on, like purlins, rafters, ridge boards, wall plates, battens and joists. Rafters were cut at an angle at one end to join the ridge board of a roof, and notched at the other with a bird's beak cut or joint, to rest on the wall plate. Dad would measure and cut one rafter as a master or template and I would measure and mark out rafters for him to cut using his long panel saw. Eventually I tried my hand cutting the angles and the joint but it was hard work and I found it difficult to keep the cuts square, so Dad would give me thinner pieces to mark out and practice. He was very possessive about his tools that he kept in a large wooden case, like a suitcase but with a drop down side. Inside all his tools were ready to hand fitting in designated slots or spaces. In a separate long open box with a wooden carry handle and compartments, he kept an array of nails and screws. I wasn't allowed to touch either without permission. They were his livelihood but in due course we designed and built smaller versions for myself and I started my own collection of tools.

Dad said I had to design my own nail carrier, work out all the dimensions of each piece, and draw it on paper. He called it a "joiner's rod" the term used for a plan and I had several attempts before it passed muster. I was loaned a T square to mark out the sections on a plank in pencil, then go round the lines with a marking knife. I now needed a bench hook comprising a flat piece of plywood and a piece of 2x1 screwed on opposite sides and ends. Placed on a bench, one piece of 2x1 would stop the hook moving and the second piece on top became a stop to hold the piece I was cutting. I was getting impatient with all this preparatory work but Dad insisted,

"If a job was worth doing it was worth doing well." And "It'll do, won't do!"

With Dad's hand over mine on the saw he guided me through

the first cuts getting them square in two dimensions. By the time I had cut several compartment dividers and the sides and ends of the tray I was doing quite well and with the aid of two-inch oval wire nails I had it all joined together.

Inevitably, the day came for my first day at school. Mam and Grandma re-knitted some of Mam's recycled wool into pullovers and, Mam took me to the Co-op department store to kit me out with grey shorts, long grey socks, a blazer, white shirts, and a school tie. They were all two sizes too big so that I would grow into them. The only things that fitted were my shoes and I was told to look after them and not get them scuffed.

Dad came to the gate to see me off, shook my hand and wished me the best of luck and to work hard. Taking my hand, Mam walked me round to St Luke's Primary School about half a mile away. I made a good mental note of the route just in case I felt the urge to escape. Looking back at my building site, my home, my territory, my environment I felt like a fish out of water, being dragged reluctantly into the unknown. All too soon, we arrived at the iron gates to the school, mounted on square stone pillars topped with a pineapple finial on a plinth.

A low brick wall topped with double-chamfered stone copings and railings surrounded the school, and playgrounds making it look more like a prison. In some ways it was similar to the building site compounds where I was king of the castle, but now I was a stranger, an interloper in a foreign land.

The gate led to the playground and the arched double doors of a Victorian red brick single storey building, the gable end embellished with dental ornamental brickwork.

Dental ornamental brickwork

I could wax lyrical here about the features of the building but my mind was firmly focussed on the tall thin man standing in the doorway. In a dark three-piece suit adorned with a gold watch chain, round black framed spectacles and short back and sides he reminded me of a taller slimmer Mr. Simpkins but altogether leaner and meaner. He was the headmaster, a Mr. Chettle. Mam had rehearsed me to say 'Good Morning Mr. Chettle' in order to make a good first impression, but nerves got the better of me and I spluttered out "Good Morning Mr. Kettle."

"Ah you must be Walters from the building site." He observed looking down upon me. Why was I singled out just because I was from the building site? Was I different to a boy living on Mafeking Street or the greengrocer's son?

"Make your way into the hall." Mam was about to walk me in but Mr. Chettle put a hand up waving her away.

"Leave him with us Mrs. Walters."

Mam reluctantly let go of my hand and, gently pushing me forward, turned and set off at a pace for the gate. I glanced back at her to see her putting a hanky to her eyes.

The hall was of wood block parquet flooring, highly polished with a huge ornamental fireplace and buckets of coal and logs each side. I joined a gaggle of new starters stood in aimless

64

silent, anticipation as Mr. Chettle strode to the front, his leather shoes echoing on the floor. All eyes were upon him. Three teachers sat on the stage keeping a wary eye on us as Mr. Chettle climbed the steps to a lectern. He introduced himself and then named the three teachers who were to be our form teachers. I tried to find one who looked pleasant and kind but my search was in vain. They all looked rather po-faced and stern.

"When I call your name walk quickly to the front and stand in line and then your teacher will take you to your classroom".

After two classes had lined up and left I realised we were being called in alphabetical order and it looked like I was to be in Mr. Haslam's class, known infamously as "Slasher Haslam" for his injurious use of a plimsoll to instil discipline.

"Walters!"

"Walters!!"

"William Walters! Answer your name boy!!!"

I had always answered to Will or Fred or 'yer wee bassa' but never Walters and now in half an hour of starting school I had two black marks against one of my names.

Our crocodile marched off behind Mr. Haslam to our allocated desks where a sheet of paper, folded into a triangle, like a Toblerone bar, had my name written upon it. There followed an introduction to the school rules which comprised mainly of everything we could not do and the punishments that we might expect if we broke them.

There was a large cast iron radiator on the wall behind the teacher and hanging on it was a slender short cane with a curved handle, like a mini walking stick. We soon worked out what it was for, the ultimate deterrent and punishment when a slap on the head, edge of a ruler across your knuckles, the flat of the ruler across your open palm or bend over and get slippered failed to have the desired effect. Thinking back, I cannot recall anyone getting the cane or anything more than a stern rebuke or

"Go and stand in the corner facing the wall until you learn how to behave".

Occasionally a piece of chalk winged your way for talking or not paying attention.

One poor girl was so frightened that a pool of pee appeared under her desk.

"Sir, Sir," shouted the boy next to her with his hand in the air whilst pointing with the other in her direction. Directing his gaze to the poor timorous child Slasher instructed,

"Go and sit on the pipes girl until you are dry!" pointing to the six inch cast iron pipes that ran round the room, where she sat ridiculed and dejected.

I was determined to keep my pee in until playtime and it was such a relief to run down the playground to the boys' toilets that were no more than a brick wall six feet high with a narrow stone drain on the floor. In days and weeks to come this would be a competition area to see who could pee the highest.

Next to the school gate was a pile of metal milk crates holding small "third of a pint" bottles and we were all instructed to drink one on pain of death, as milk was good for us. Sometimes I managed a couple if someone didn't like milk. At morning playtime a teacher would stand by the milk crates to ensure everybody drank one bottle and no-one drank two. You had to bring a note from your Mam if you did not like it but some would just take a bottle and give it away.

The teacher held a packet of biscuits for the better off kids to buy a couple for a penny or two. I always had a good breakfast so managed to save my pennies.

Mr. Chettle rang the prison bell, just like Mr. Simpkins and it was back to class.

At dinnertime, we were crocodiled to trestle tables in the main hall. Each table had a number and we were called in order to march to the serving hatch to be handed a plate of dinner. No choice, take it leave it. Swilled down with a glass of water and followed by a second march for your pudding, jam sponge and custard, but not like Mam makes.

The afternoon included a quiet period where we all had to put our arms on the desk as a pillow for our heads and have a nap, but I used the time to peek out and see what everyone else was doing. I caught the eye of the girl who wet her knickers and gave her a smile, which she returned. I had made a friend.

Mam was at the gate to meet me. She was overjoyed to see me yet, worried in case I was upset. I held her hand tightly as I skipped along recounting my day. As the days and weeks passed, I grew accustomed to the school rules, and how to bend them. I did well in my strong subjects that happened to be the Three Rs, reading writing and arithmetic, along with art. I wasn't too bothered about religious education but I did enjoy music, geography and history. My fearless athletic prowess and agility in the gymnasium owed everything to a lifetime of swinging from scaffolding and running along narrow beams. I was a natural.

It was a great shock to me to find that there was so much more out there in the real world than I had ever imagined in my little kingdom. So much to learn.

But on the home front there was an almost total reduction in my income from doing errands and getting a free pie or potato fritter. If there was overtime on the site on Saturdays, I managed a few jobs for the workers but also found many collectables on my weekend forays. So much so that my store was overflowing and Dad said we needed to do something about it. The following Friday Mr. Clelland turned up in his Jaguar with the ever-present Miss Primly who asked if Mr. Clelland could call and see me. I felt most honoured and proud that he wanted to see me. But whatever for?

"Now William I understand that you have been gathering all the waste nails and things dropped on the site? Could I have a look at what you have got?"

I was dumbfounded and took him to my stash of National Dried Milk tins and few odd boxes I had made.

"Mmmm! That's a fair old collection William. What do you plan to do with it all?"

"Err, I don't know Mr. Clelland. I don't know anyone who wants to buy it."

"That's your problem William. You don't have a market for your products. A good businessman should always find a market, somewhere to sell his goods. I tell you what, how about I offer you £5 for all your stock. I can put it all back in the stores to be used again. A good businessman must keep an eye on what is being wasted, cut down on costs and using your collection I can work out the total wastage on all my building sites".

I nodded knowingly at his advice but stunned at his offer that I readily agreed.

"I would like you to write me a list of everything you have, let's call it an invoice, and deliver the goods to the site office. How's that for an idea?"

I nodded.

"You see what happens when you look after your pennies William – they turn into pounds. Let's shake hands on our deal".

I was overjoyed at the thought of £5 for my Post Office account but the celebration was rather muted when I got some further sobering advice from Mr. Clelland.

"William". He had my full attention.

"When you sell something or buy something you need to negotiate the price and never accept the first offer made to you. You have to bargain. Try to get more for your goods. Or, if you are buying, try to pay less for them. Once you agree a price and shake hands that's a Gentleman's agreement, a contract and you have to stick with it".

I was left a little perplexed and then realised that I might have got a bit more out of

Mr. Clelland so was slightly disappointed at what I might have got. On the other hand, maybe I had received valuable advice and learnt a lesson. Maybe Archy and I needed to rethink what we charged for running errands.

ROMEO AND JULIA

My new school friend was Julia Jackson, small and slim with long mousey-blonde hair held to one side with a colourful bow and resembling a china doll. I sensed from our first day in school that, like me, she was a bit of a loner. Yes, I was a loner as well. I had the company of the men on the site and Archy and I knew some of the boys in the street, but only through the compound fence. As the classes were alphabetical I had less contact with Archiy Armour in class one, As to Ds, and I was the other end of the alphabet in class three with the Js to Zs. Luckily Julia had just scraped into my life.

All my life I had only socialised with grown-ups and found it easier to talk to them than children. I had never played all the childhood games of my peers nor was I able to speak their language or converse about the things they knew about.

Julia had an all together different upbringing. At the turn of the 19th century, her great grandfather and his brother started a tinsmith business on the outskirts of the town. Operating from an old farm building and a large yard on a main road out of town they would cut, roll, fold, solder and rivet tin and other white metals into boxes and tins of all shapes and sizes; as well as candle moulds and holders, stovepipes and guttering, buckets and water pitchers. Gradually over the decades, the town expanded its housing away from the long rows of red brick back-to-back terraces into semi-detached and detached villas in brick and stone with front and rear gardens and inside toilets. There was a desire to leave the smoky overcrowded industrial heart of the town and look for better healthier places to live in the fresh clean air of the suburbs.

Jacksons built a small shop on their site stocking it with all the hardware needs of an ever-growing number of new neighbours wanting a local shop rather than getting a bus or tram into town. I suppose it was the start of DIY as people took a pride in their new homes and wanted to improve the interiors and their gardens. The shop now brimmed with buckets, brooms, mops, brushes of all kinds, soaps, detergents, Dolly Blue to make your whites look whiter and disinfectants, paraffin from a hand operated bowser outside, candles and tools. In fact, it was so full that customers had to squeeze down the overflowing aisles to reach the counter where shelves were laden with labelled cardboard boxes. Nothing was very expensive but Mr Jackson's advice and knowledge were valued and invaluable when it came to setting rat and mouse traps, hanging shelves or plumbing a sink.

The shop grew and grew with their reputation and they had customers coming from all over the town. The old farmyard and tinsmith workshop was cleared to build a warehouse for their stock but as trade and the demand for different goods grew like paint, lighting and wallpaper they needed a larger shop that filled the frontage onto the busy arterial road with lots of passing trade.

Julia's father was the third generation of "Tinny Jacksons" as they were known by the townspeople, and having prospered, he was a leading light in the Chamber of Trade. Julia's mother was a local lass leaving school to be a shop assistant at the store leading to the inevitable relationship with her father. They now occupied a new stone-built end-of-three terrace, three-bedroom villa in a leafy cul-de-sac, complete with bathroom and toilet. The front garden was bordered by a stone wall, and a straight path led from the wrought iron gate to the front door. Either side of the path was a lawn edged with herbaceous borders. It was definitely posh compared to our pre-fab and to the two-up-two-downs around the building site. Mrs Jackson was keen to divorce herself from her early life and surroundings and focussed her efforts on being a social climber, developing new "better class" friends. She enjoyed the functions put on by the Chamber of Trade and the opportunity to hobnob with the great and good of the town, business people, industrialists and so on. She was always immaculately dressed, not a hair out of place and powder and lipstick regularly refreshed.

In some respects, Julia was a demonstration of her mother's successful rise in society and not allowed to mix with the more common children in the area, nor get her beautiful clothes dirty playing in the park or nearby fields. There was absolutely no possibility of her playing on a building site or being exposed to Glaswegian slang. Just imagine her going home and telling mother that this strange man from another world yelled "yur wee bassa!" You may now understand why Julia felt so isolated and estranged at school, timorous and mouse-like, daring not to speak.

The second day at school started with assembly standing in rows singing hymns to a piano played by the music teacher. Mr. Chettle led prayers. My parents were not religious sorts or God-botherers, Dad was christened Catholic and mother was Methodist but they only went to church for weddings and funerals. When Dad spoke to the priest at the Catholic Church about reading the Banns for their wedding, the priest suggested he should wait till a good Catholic girl came along.

"Too late for that Father, if you know what I mean!"

The priest nodded knowingly.

"Ah the sins of the flesh. So be it. When did you last come to confession?""

Any road up, they married at the registry office instead and that is why I never went to Sunday School. Assembly was CofE, Church of England as required by the local education authority and all the other faiths had to like it or lump it.

Mr. Chettle gave out school notices or news,

"There is an outbreak of nits at another school so get your mothers to check your head for creepy crawlies".

That meant a good raking with a nit comb looking for eggs, the nits, or live insects. It was odd that people with clean hair seemed to get them more than the dirty oichs or was that an old wives' tale? Sometimes it was body lice feeding off your blood and you looked suspiciously at anyone scratched at their clothing. Mostly it was about bad behaviour, running in the corridors, slamming doors, sliding down the banisters, being late for school and failing to wash hands before dinner. Occasionally there was some good news like an extra half day off school or recognition for good work.

From the second day, Julia and I formed a relationship. I looked for her through the school railings as I arrived and saw a green van pull outside the gates carrying Mr. and Mrs. Jackson and Julia. Mother straightened Julia's coat and dress, brushed her hair with her hand and placed her new satchel over her head, kissing her on the forehead. Julia seemed to turn reluctantly towards the school as the van door slammed but saw me through the railings and instantly her sad face became a beaming smile as she skipped through the gate. We were so far apart socially and in our life experiences that it was difficult to find something in common to talk about. But, we found interest in those uncommon things, our families, our environment, favourite foods, and soon we were chatting as if we had known each other for years.

Julia nipped to the toilet before class and she survived the day dry and unashamed. She was not the only child that had accidents, especially after milk break, so she realised she was not alone in her suffering.

Chatting was not allowed in class on pain of a piece of flying chalk or the ruler so we re-assured each other with glances and quick smiles when "Slasher" was writing on the board. Teachers seemed to have a third eye in the back of their heads, seeing or sensing that someone was talking and whipping round to fling the chalk, or make you stand up to answer a question. You needed to have your wits about you and be ready with a reply, so no problem for a cheeky blighter from the building site. Sometimes we would write notes but that was filled with danger. There was always someone ready to blab to the teacher,

"Sir. Sir, Walters is writing to Julia".

"Bring me the note, Walters". I would march forward trying to look ashamed and about to be admonished, hand over the note and start to return to my seat,

"Wait!"

Slasher read the note and almost smiled. "I agree Walters. Back to your seat."

It was a set up.

"Class! Walters has written that he is enjoying this geography lesson and would like to travel round the world. I trust you are all enjoying the lesson as well?" There was dumbfounded silence.

"Well are you enjoying the lesson?"

"Yes Mr. Haslam." They responded in that drawling way that children do.

Julia and I enjoyed that experience but were more careful in future, especially now we knew there was a clackfart [Derbyshire slang for tell-tale or blabber] ready to inform on us, but I had ways of getting my own back. One morning I arrived at school early and was by the door ready to enter as soon as the bell rang. I was first in the classroom and slipped a little package into the blabber's desk. The first lesson was natural history with Miss Woodhouse, an older lady dressed in musty tweeds and a pink twin-set jumper and cardigan.

"Miss! Miss!" I exclaimed with my hand raised.

"Can't you wait for the toilet?"

"Not that Miss. I can hear a strange noise like a scratching sound".

Miss Woodhouse walked over to investigate tilting her best ear to one side listening intently.

"There it is again Miss!"

"Where boy? Where?"

"It sounds like it is in a desk Miss".

"Right, all of you open your desks".

She was standing next to Clackfart as he opened his lid and out popped the head of a house mouse.

Miss Woodhouse screamed, "Get it out! Get it out!"

For once Clackfart was speechless, coughing and spluttering that it was not his mouse. Several girls shrieked jumping to safety on their chairs. Miss Woodhouse took hold of his ear thrusting him through the classroom door with instructions to wait outside Mr. Chettle's office.

Walters came to the rescue with a small cardboard box adeptly scooping the poor creature up and away.

"Outside! Outside with it!" commanded Miss Woodhouse.

I returned triumphantly past the distraught Blabber to receive a hero's welcome and a cheer from the class and Miss Woodhouse. It is not always possible to win a war outright or change the school rules but it was good to achieve a small victory now and again.

School life was pretty much as you would expect, enjoying some subjects more than others. In a free lesson or art, I would draw plans or joiners rods for my projects using my geometry set purchased in Scarborough. With income dwindling to almost nothing, I needed a new product and Miss Woodhouse was my inspiration and sponsor. We had guinea pigs in the school so I drew up a joiner's rod for a complicated two-storey house with ramps and an exercise wheel. Dad suggested changes to the rod on Friday evening and then took me to his bedroom, opened the wardrobe door and removed a brown hessian almost semi-circular heavy-duty bag, a bit like a shopping bag but with brass eyelets and rope handles. Fixing his eyes on me, Dad lifted it on to the kitchen table causing the weighty contents to rattle and clunk.

I was desperate to see the contents. I knew what the bag was because I had seen joiners use them on site, but what was in it?

"Now Fred", Dad started in a serious tone,

"This was your granddad's tool bass and he gave it to me when I started work and gradually over the years I replaced his tools with new ones. I believe it is time to pass his tools on to you so you can make good use of them. It's no good them lying in the bottom of the wardrobe".

Dad opened the bass out to reveal lovely old chisels, saws, screwdrivers, squares, even an odd pencil, in fact everything I needed to make hutches.

"Look at the tools with wooden handles Fred and you will see Granddad's initials stamped on them. The metal ones will have a mark filed on the shaft to identify them as Frederick Walters".

"That's lucky as I don't have to stamp my initials. I can use F.W. just like Granddad".

"Pick them up Fred. Feel them in your hand. Feel their history, the places they have been, the things they have made. Feel your Granddad's sweat on the wood".

My goodness! Dad was really waxing lyrical and getting a bit emotional, but the longer I held them, caressed them, stroked them the more I could feel his father's presence in my hand.

"Fred, I have looked after them, sharpened them so they are all ready to use. Remember a sharp chisel cuts wood but a blunt one only cuts flesh". I put the tenon saw gently back in the bass and gave Dad a big long hug. "Can we make a joiner's case like yours?"

"Your granddad made that for me when I started work and it has served me well all these years. Of course we can make one for you to fit all these tools in".

Dad suggested changes to the rod on Friday evening, I stayed up redrawing the plans, and cutting lists ready to start work on Saturday morning. With Archy in attendance, finding and

fetching scrap timber, we completed the hutch ready for Miss Woodhouse's lesson on Monday morning. I was extremely proud of our joint efforts as we marched into the playground attracting a lot of interest. Julia helped me carry it to our classroom entering before the bell to set it up. Miss Woodhouse and Mr. Chettle were so pleased that it merited a mention on school notices at assembly. I was seldom out of work after that with requests for rabbit hutches, nest boxes for chickens and, bird tables. I was back in the money and
Mr. Clelland would have been pleased as punch that I had found or created a new market.

Julia and I were very fortunate that we had similar ability levels so avoided separation when pupils were streamed into groups like top maths and bottom English. We were in top streams for most subjects. Julia was top group for music, which was not my forte, but she was having private piano lessons at home. Her mother gave her the choice of ballet classes or the piano. Boys and girls did separate PE and played different games, rounders and netball for the girls, football and cross-country for the boys. Cross-country amounted to running round the boundary of our small sports field when the football pitch was a mud bath. In bad weather, we did circuit training in the main hall, climbing wooden wall bars and the ropes hanging from a sliding track on the ceiling. On the ground, we ran along low benches, jumped over the vaulting horse, clambered from one end to the other of the pommel horse, did press-ups and picked up the heavy suede medicine balls. I was totally in my element. I was back on my building site shimmying up scaffold poles and swinging from beams, getting A+ on my reports.

However, it did look like other factors were about to play a part in separating Julia and me. The building site had been a massive construction project but work was due for completion in a year or even a matter of months. I heard Mam and Dad talking about what they would do next, where they might end up and moving house.

Mam was ready for a move as the pre-fab was now rather worse for wear and she wanted a proper home on a street or even a leafy cul-de-sac. I had seen the look in her eyes when I described Julia's house and I know she had been past for a secret envious glance at her aspiration.

Julia and I were upset at the thought of being apart, especially if Dad was moved to a new site far away, but in the absence of anything definite there was nothing we could do about it except hope. Grandma always used to say, "You can live in Hope even if you die in Castleton". Two Derbyshire villages situated next to each other in the Peak District. So we lived in hope and I kept my ear close to the ground, or Mam and Dad's bedroom wall for any snippet of information.

The answer came in a telephone call from Miss Primly to my Dad asking him to attend Mr. Clelland's office on Friday morning. This was not uncommon, so we had no reason to think it was about leaving the site. Miss Primly showed Dad into Mr. Clelland's office taking orders for tea while the men discussed the latest news from the site.

The office was like Miss Primly, tidy, everything in its place, efficient but unlike Miss Primly smelt of floor polish and leather. Mr Clelland's huge leather-topped mahogany desk sat in the centre on a square rug. He sat on a Captain's swivel chair, also in mahogany with a padded maroon leather seat and back and five legs on castors. There was little on his desk apart from a large blotting paper pad, ink and pen stand and a set of in/out trays. Dad noticed a brown manila file on the pad.

Mr. Clelland asked about Mam and Fred.

"Still collecting nails is he?"

Dad informed him about my new entrepreneurial ventures and Mr. Clelland was delighted I had followed his advice to find new products and markets.

"Anyway Jimmy. Let's get down to business...."

Mr. Clelland thought the site would be sorted in about six months leaving just the redevelopment of the compounds into car parks.

"So we need to find a new place for you Jimmy".

Dad feared the worst being shifted to a new site, possibly in the north east or even the Home Counties. He had kept his ear to the ground working out what new developments were on the cards and prepared his answers in readiness.

Mr. Clelland opened the file and started turning the pages.

"Jimmy. You have made a great success of your site, a happy workforce, low turnover, few accidents, no fatalities, low snagging, low waste and pilfering, you work well with suppliers and above all the quality of the build is excellent. If only all our sites were operated like yours."

Dad was feeling quite pumped up by such recognition of his achievements but anticipated a pin to prick his bubble.

"Jimmy...." Mr. Clelland paused looking Dad straight in the eye....

"I have a new job for you. It's a new role in the company. I want you as a regional manager going to sites and getting them to work like your site. I want you as a trouble-shooter. I want you to train existing managers and find the best up-and-coming chaps to be site managers".

Dad started to respond but was rather taken aback having not prepared any responses in readiness.

"Let me finish Jimmy. It would mean working from here at head office and travelling to sites, sometimes stopping there a few days. You would have an expense account, of course, for hotels and meals and a new car. Oh, a significant increase in wages, salaried of course, that means a proper pension when you retire. What do you think Jimmy?"

Dad was gobsmacked. Flabbergasted. His brain was trying to take it all in racing from one consideration to another, housing, school for me, financial security, his ability to do the job. But Mr. Clelland would not have made the offer if Jimmy was not up to it.

Mr. Clelland continued to watch every movement on Jimmy's face and his body language. "Come on Jimmy you have been in far more difficult spots than this. Nobody is shooting at you or trying to blow you up. You are not entering a minefield. This is a chance to make something of your life, a chance you deserve through your endeavour and hard work. You have all the qualities and more to do this job. I would not offer it if I thought for one second you were not capable".

There was a long pause.

"Well Mr. Clelland there is a lot to think about and I would want to discuss it with Vee but I think the answer would be …..yes".

"You can tell Vee that there is a moving allowance to cover carpets and curtains and you will need a spare room for an office with a telephone and that the firm will pay all expenses. That way you don't have to come into the office every day. Work from home. Travel to the sites. How does that sound?"

"Sounds terrific Mr. Clelland. Just terrific".

"Joa er Miss Primly, I think a sherry is in order or even a whiskey to celebrate our new regional manager".

The two settled down to talk through some finer details and finish their celebratory tipple and Miss Primly, smiled warmly, handed Dad a thick envelope containing his new contract and Dad nodded his appreciation.

Mam was staggered at the news; ecstatic, elated, euphoric, overjoyed until the practicalities of buying a house and moving started to bring her down to earth. Dad wiped away her tears of joy as they sat down to work out their future together. I sensed something strange when I got in from school, both looking at me rather oddly.

I was just as surprised and shocked as Mam and jumped up and down with joy and excitement until I thought about leaving Archy and above all, Julia. I was anxious where we would live. Dad reassured me that we would have a new, proper house in the town, but in a better area so I would still see my friends and continue my schooling. What a relief. I could not wait until the next morning to meet Julia as she climbed out her father's van. There was barely enough time to reveal all before the bell went, but by the end of the day we had discussed everything we could think of and happy to be staying close together.

The Blabber was a continuing nuisance and a bully. Although he was taller and more heavily-built than me, he was flabby and slow on his toes, so he picked on the smaller kids. He cheated them at marbles or "mobdies" as we called them, persuading them to handover sweets and sometimes a few pennies. He had no friends and was not very good at anything other than throwing his weight around. I came upon him one day round a corner by the dustbins holding a younger boy by the collar and demanding sweets. His right arm was raised ready to slap or punch the boy but he had not reckoned on me creeping up behind him and taking his wrist as he was about to strike. I whipped his arm round and up his back making him squeal and my left hand held him across his chest and under his chin so he could not move. He howled in protest but I pulled his left ear towards me and whispered some words of advice about changing his ways. Or else! The bully was a coward and he ran off blubbering and blurting threats of vengeance about setting his brother on me. He was a spent force, certainly, when I was in his presence. It soon got round the school about the Blabber being reduced to tears by yours truly and I was treated with great respect and regard.

Julia and I had eagerly awaited our 11 plus exam results hoping to go to the senior school together. I kept watch on the postman turning the corner and crossing towards the crude letterbox in the compound fence, and snatching it from his hand from the inside. Mam and Dad were at breakfast as I presented the brown envelope to them with both sets of fingers crossed behind my back. Dad wiped the butter and marmalade off his knife and slit the envelope slowly and carefully, almost teasing me as he removed a piece of paper that would affect the rest of my life. Mam kicked him under the table to get on with it. Dad smiled and handed the letter to Mam. "Grammar school. You got Grammar School. Oh well done Fred. Look!" Sure enough, I was on my way to the boy's grammar school. My next thought was Julia as we had agreed to meet in the park near her home. I waited on the roundabout for what seemed an age until I saw her enter the park gates. Julia waved and started running towards me. Like me, Julia was destined for the grammar school for girls at the other side of town. Luckily we both travelled into the town centre on a free bus pass, and then out again to our respective schools. It would have made sense for boys and girls to be together and eventually that is what happened.

In the meantime, we would meet after school for a coffee in the bus station cafe or just walk round the shops until it was time to head home and get our homework done. I think we were both rather sad parting after such brief times together but they made weekends and holidays so much more special.

DAYLIGHT ROBBERY

It was nearing the end of our last summer term at junior school, the 11 plus had streamed our classes into grammar school or secondary modern starting in September. The last week at school was very free-and-easy with little schoolwork. Wednesday was the obligatory sports day with parents participating in sack races and the egg and spoon sprint, and Mothers had a special race running 60 yards tossing a pancake in a frying pan. Thursday morning was prize giving for the sports and academic achievements throughout the year, with sporting cups for the school teams but mostly book tokens for the top three in various subjects.

By dinnertime we were at least free to go home with the rest of the day off. Archy and me changed into our scruffs and assumed our favourite spot in the crow's nest. It was all fairly quiet with little or no activity in the street or on the site as it prepared to close down for builder's holiday fortnight.

To the right of the site car park was a long ginnel, snicket or alleyway running the full length of the site joining the street in the front of the site to the main road at the rear. It was a regular cut through for pedestrians and bikes, even motor bikes, and although wide enough to drive a small van along it, the opening onto our street was blocked by a single concrete bollard. Occasionally we had seen locals drive all the way up and then have to back their way out. And so it was, that we heard a vehicle approaching from the main road end coming to a stop just in front of the bollard, but on this occasion two men got out, unloaded two sledgehammers from the back of the van and started to pound the bollard.

Archy and I thought we ought to investigate.

I said, "Let's play footie in the ginnel and see what they are doing".

After kicking around on the street we entered the ginnel and started kicking against the wall where Archy was in goal. The rear doors to the dark blue Ford Transit van were open and I could see that there were none of the usual tools you would expect a builder to have, no picks or shovels, trowels or buckets just a handful of pick-axe handles. When the men weren't paying any attention I and booted the ball into the back of the van and shouted,

"Goal! Liverpool one, Everton nil." In my best scouse accent,

"'Ere mister our ball went in your van can we get it?"

The men looked up from their labours struggling to remove the concrete chunks from the four thick strands of metal reinforcing rod. One of them dropped the hammer and walked silently almost menacingly to the back of the van.

"Get it out". He growled in a strange accent and went back to the bollard muttering to his mate.

Emboldened, two curious kids asked why they were knocking it down.

The other man stood up to reveal a Chelsea shirt under his donkey jacket.

"Council wants it replacing as its dangerous". He had the same accent as the other man. I went on another tack.

"Are you a Chelsea fan then? We are Liverpool and Everton".

He was about to continue the conversation when the other man interrupted telling him to get on with the job.

"Now clear off kids".

It was all very odd. For a start, they didn't have any tools, nothing to cut the metal bars and no real reason for doing it. Archy and

I kept watch a bit longer. The men did not try to cut the rods and just bent it back and forth until it lay flat on the ground and then driving over it into the street. The other odd thing was they had NCB in white letters on the back of their donkey jackets and everybody knows up north that NCB means National Coal Board and nothing to do with the council.

Dad was very interested and cross-examined us closely about the details and description of the van.

"Pity you didn't get the number" he said.

I held out my open palm to reveal the number written in Biro.

"I didn't have any paper".

"Well done Fred. Stick your hand on the photocopier. That'll do, but better not wash it off for a while. Now go and have tea and cake with your Mam while I make a couple of calls".

Any road up, Dad called the Trilbies and the local CIDs. About an hour later, the Trilbies and two lookalikes from the CID arrived at Dad's office and we had to give our account all over again. They were very interested. When they had gone Dad told me and Archy that we must not say anything to anyone, not even Julia, until we were told otherwise, stressing it was very important.

The next morning Mam roused me from my bed early with instructions to get washed and dressed as we were going out. This was most odd especially without any explanation, but I could tell from her manner and tone that she was worried. Shortly after, there was a knock at the door and in walked Archy and his mother. I mouthed, "What's up?" Archy shrugged his shoulders. A quick check on the cleanliness of our ears, a brush of my hair and a check on my school uniform and we were whisked off the site, again most unusual as Archy walked to school.

Crossing the road we took a left turn away from the school as Mam gripped my hand tighter to prevent any escape, quickening her pace. I kept looking at Archy who was just as bemused as me.

A young woman stood smoking about fifty yards away and on seeing us, dropped her cigarette and walked towards us.

"Mrs Williams? Mrs Armour" she enquired. The Mams nodded.

"And this must be William and Archy". We nodded.

"Follow me please".

A few streets further away we turned into an archway called Theatre Yard, the back entrance to the police station where all the cars and bikes were parked.

Theatre Yard

This was all very cloak and dagger stuff. On the far side of the yard was a metal fire escape leading to the first floor. Our mams pushed us forward to follow the lady through the door into a large office full of desks and mostly men in plain clothes. Whisking us into a small side room, the lady explained that we were in the main CID office at the police station and that we were to stay here for a couple of hours and she would explain more later.

"What about some tea and a bit of breakfast? Follow me".

Police Station

The station was built in the early thirties in brick and stone and was originally a police station and a fire station. We echoed along a long gloss-painted corridor turning into a side room signed "Canteen". There was no need for a sign as Archy and I could have tracked it down by the smell of bacon and sausages wafting down the corridor.

"Now what would you like. You can have anything. You are our guests". Our mams just had a pot of tea and poached egg on toast but we had the full monty, sausage and bacon, fried egg and tomatoes and a slice of black pudding with toast and jam.

"By eck! These two can't half put it away" she said.

"Better walk that lot down so how about a tour of the police station?"

We descended by the back stairs into an enormous garage with four sets of high folding doors.

"This is where the fire engines were kept".

Crossing the garage we entered a corridor into the main police station,

"Let's look in here. This is where they receive calls for breakdowns and emergencies on the M1". Two ladies sat behind a bank of plugs, cables and sockets on the station switchboard, answering callers, pulling out a cable and plugging them into an extension. They were very busy with calls and soon the board looked like a bowl of red spaghetti. Behind them was a map of the motorway showing the location of the emergency telephones.

Passing the main entrance, we came to the charge office where prisoners were documented.

"Just get the cell keys Sarge if that's ok?" The Sergeant looked up from his paperwork and nodded. Across the corridor and through the door marked cells, we followed our guide into a dim stark cold tiled room with concrete floors leading to two corridors, one for men and the other for females, lined with cells. On the male side there were four heavy-duty doors, obviously thick wood plated with steel set in steel frames in the brick walls. A sliding metal hatch allowed the gaoler to look in on his captive clients. Our gaoler pushed the door open and beckoned us to enter quickly slamming the door behind us with a bang. Our Mams were at the hatch declaring this would be ideal for keeping us out of trouble. A small barred window let in a little light but, there was nothing in the cell apart from a solid wooden bed and a steel toilet with no seat just a wooden rim bolted to the rim.

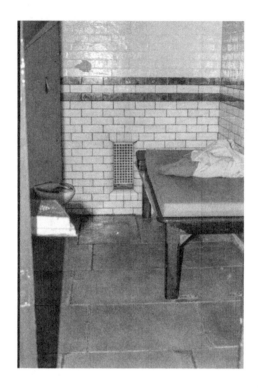

Police Cell

We were pleased to be released from custody and breathe the fresh air in the rear yard where two police officers in uniform with white caps were waiting to demonstrate a patrol car and motorcycle. This was more like it, sitting on the bike flashing the blue lights and tooting the two tones.

"I suppose that as you are in police custody you should be photographed and fingerprinted" said our tour guide, marching us along the main corridor to the sound of police radio coming from a hatch in the wall.

We had schoolmates with tellies who told us about Z Cars and we would play cops and robbers just like Z-Victor One, but this was the real thing. Archy and I paused at the hatch to "Hang a tab on."

"Come along boys they are busy in the control at the moment." Our guide instructed in a tone not to be ignored.

"Follow me please."

I looked through the hatch at the radio operator behind his console with the Superintendent standing behind him.

The top of the main staircase led to the Scene of Crime office. A nice gentleman in plain clothes, called Mr. Sowery, welcomed us, scanning our open palms paying particular attention to the tips of our fingers.

"Oh yes you have whorls and you have double loops. Every fingerprint is unique and if a criminal touches something at the scene of his crime, he leaves his fingerprint. My job is to find his fingerprints at the scene and match them with our records". He had our fullest attention.

"Just touch this piece of glass with your index finger". He demonstrated with outstretched finger.

Opening a small jar of grey metallic dust he dipped a soft brush and stoked the glass lightly to reveal in great detail our whorl and double loop. Magic.

"I want you to write your names on these forms".

The forms contained a series of boxes, one for each finger and thumb. As we filled in our names, he dabbed ink from a tube on a copper plate and rolled it until the plate was black. Fixing a form under a wooden clamp and taking my hand and a finger, he rolled my finger tip to leave a square-shaped impression of my whorls.

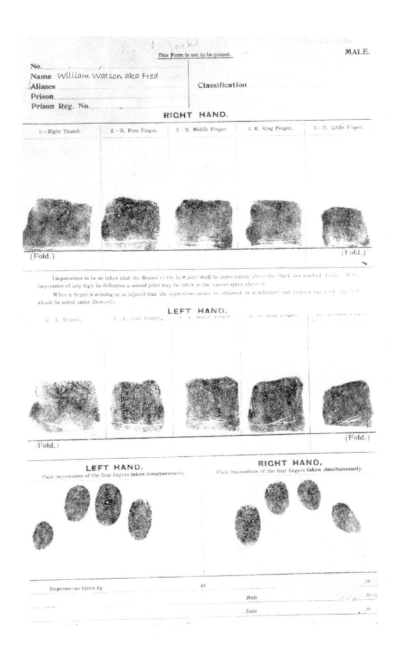

A new rag and some methylated spirits followed by soap and water restored our hands to the satisfaction of our Mams. Across the end of the room was a single wooden chair bolted to the floor in front of a large wide sheet of thick paper hanging from a roll attached to the ceiling. A camera sat on a tripod in front of it.

The chair looked most uncomfortable, no padding, a flat seat and a strip of wood running from front to back right under your bottom.

"That's to make you sit up straight" the photographer said. Times many the teachers had told us to sit up straight but thank heavens we did not have a strip of wood to sit on.

"Look straight at the camera please. You are not under arrest so you can smile you know". Flash.

"Swivel right please". Flash

"Swivel all the way to the left please". Flash

"Thank you. Now the next one".

All done we were informed the photos would be ready in about an hour.

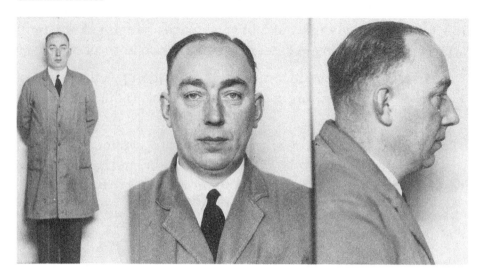

Typical Mug Shot

How long were we going to be there and why were we there?

"Do you lads play table tennis?" the guide asked trooping us up to the top floor

We entered a social area with a bar and darts board and up some steps to a hall marked out for badminton. We played table tennis while the three ladies sat in deep conversation. Archy and me played for a while and then tried the darts board whispering and trying to work it all out. The photographer appeared with our mug shots still warm from the processor and we thanked him for his lesson and the pictures.

After he left, the phone rang and our host said,

"That's great. Fantastic news". She approached with a smile as big as the Mersey tunnel.

"I can tell you now what this is all about. Let's get a cup of tea".

We gathered round a table in the canteen in great anticipation.

"Yesterday you came across two men in a van knocking down a bollard in the ginnel". We nodded enthusiastically

"Those two men were known criminals from London".

"I knew they were not from up north by their funny accent and that Chelsea football shirt" I exclaimed.

"The number you wrote on your hand was correct but it was a false number on a stolen van. Yesterday evening officers searched the area and found it in the car park of a travel hotel just outside town. Undercover officers found the two men you described and two more so they kept observations on them. It was obvious they were up to no good and whatever they planned must be connected with the bollard in the ginnel".

We hung with baited breath on her every word.

"You know that today the builders break up for their holidays, and that it is also pay day. But they get their holiday pay as well so double wages". The day was dawning.

"The van was followed from the hotel to the street outside the building site and as the four men got out of the van wearing balaclavas and carrying pick-axe handles the police pounced".

"Did they have a right good punch up Miss?" asked Archiy in a state of extreme excitement.

"They certainly tried hard to resist but three of them were quickly overpowered. The driver sped off and turned down your ginnel, obviously their getaway route, but we had a police car parked at the other end and he was immediately blocked in and arrested. A few streets away we also found a stolen Jaguar which we believe was their getaway vehicle back to London".

We asked lots of questions but she avoided giving any further details.

"But why are we here?" I pleaded

We thought it best that you be kept here safe and sound in case there was any serious trouble". she explained.

Now it all became clear.

"What about Dad and Mrs Blackett who does the wages?"

"We kept them in a safe place as well and everyone is fine. No-one was hurt".

The canteen phone rang. "Yes Sir. Ok. Great. Be with you in a couple of minutes, Sir. Come on boys one last thing to do".

All along the main corridor, staff and police officers stood in the open doorways. At the far end the grand spiral staircase was crowded with more police officers and all the CID blocked the corridor in front of us as they broke into a rapturous applause. The door marked Superintendent opened at the end of the corridor and a man resplendent in full uniform, whistle chain and medal ribbons came out to address us.

"William and Archy. You have done this town a great service. Your actions yesterday led to the arrest of four dangerous armed criminals from London. You prevented a serious robbery from being committed and the probability of someone being seriously injured. Those four gangsters are now locked up in police cells and will go to prison for a long time". He started clapping and everyone cheered and clapped.

"Well that was a day to remember and back at the site we went over all the details again with Dad and Mr. Armour, while two relieved mothers made the evening meal and we celebrated together.

UXBS

The building site was vast and would take six or more years to complete the demolition of streets of Victorian red brick back-to-back terraces, once considered as a huge improvement on the slums of the times with many families sharing one outside toilet, no running water and people surviving in squalid, filthy, disease-ridden conditions. The new houses certainly were an improvement with a privy in the back yard, a tin bath hung on the wall and a cold-water tap in the kitchen. Four rooms, two-up-two-down for one family were never enough when many families had a newborn every year. My own great grandfather was one of fifteen who survived into adulthood. There was no National Health Service and the doctor would only come if you could pay his fee. Many died in infancy from disease and poor nutrition and no healthcare, young children worked alongside their mothers in the mills and mines to earn enough to survive.

But now, these once desirable residences were also declared as slums, rat infested, leaking, uninhabitable and the residents moved to new estates on the edge of the town. The area around the compounds was getting towards completion but the far end still had a couple of terraces left to be demolished. These were being flattened and the ground scraped clear for the diggers to start on new foundations, not just houses but a community with a school, shops and pubs.

One Sunday, Archy and I thought we should venture to the far side and see if there were any rich pickings, especially timber for our projects. The demolition men had opened up a couple of houses removing the boards sealing the doors and windows. Access to one house meant we could go upstairs and climb into the false roof or cock loft and drop into one house after the other. We always made a lot of noise when we were there because plenty of locals were on the prowl in search of lead pipe and flashing to sell at the scrap merchants.

Each house had a yard with a coalhouse and toilet. We always gave the toilets a miss as they were often full of you know what, but the coalhouse might reveal an odd tool. It didn't take us long to check a yard then leap over the wall into the next one. There was little or nothing of any value in the houses, broken chairs a few pots and bottles, remnants of the past occupants, so as a last resort we found a ladder and climbed into the cock loft. Dark and filthy dirty it was and not an easy place to search, but, who knows what the residents may have stashed away there years ago. Again nothing much, but on our return there was a glint in the beam of our torches, from a metal cylinder about a foot or so long.

"Might be worth a bit as scrap aluminium", declared Archy "It's corroded look, but not rusty".

He was right. One end was flat but the other had small fins.

"Looks like a little bomb Archy" I said warily,

"Put that down gently! It is an incendiary bomb!"

Archy did as instructed. "Will it blow the house up?"

"Not likely. In the war, they were dropped to start fires but if it goes off now we are for it. Better get out of here sharpish!" And we legged it back home to tell Dad.

Incendiary Bomb

Dad was not surprised saying they found them all the time, but they needed handling with care in case they went off. Dad had dealt with them many times, and he rang the police who sent for the Army bomb disposal. The police arrived first, taping off the entry to the house and leaving an officer there all night to keep trespassers away. The next morning, about eight o'clock, a white Landrover marked with Bomb Disposal and "jam butty" stripes arrived with a Corporal and a Private in Army uniform. Dad gave them a run down over a mug of tea and a few tales about his time as a Sapper. The two soldiers sauntered over to the house and placed the bomb in a hole on the site. Dad drove the digger over to them with a few sandbags in the bucket and then retreated to a safe distance. The soldiers walked towards us un-reeling a long cable from the hole. The Private collected a box from the Landrover with a handle and a plunger and two screw terminals on it.

The Corporal noting our intense interest enquired, "I suppose your Dad has told you all about blowing things up?"

"Not half." I blurted excitedly, "He blew a lot of things up in the war".

"Do you want to blow this one up?"

Too right I did.

With the wires connected to the terminals, he wound the handle to generate a current and pulled the top T-shaped handle out of the box.

"We are ready, so we need to check it is all clear and give the signal". The Private checked the site and gave three blasts on a compressed air siren.

"Right William and Archy I want you to put a hand each on the ends of the T bar and shout "Firing" as loud as you can and then push hard on the handle.

"Firing!" We shouted with great gusto and plunged the handle.

The result was a bit of an anti climax. There was a small bang, more of a phut than a bang really, and a jet of sand about four feet in the air followed by smoke and flames.

After, I said to Dad that it was a bit of a damp squib but he explained that the so called damp squibs were dropped in their thousands indiscriminately setting fire to many houses and killing their unsuspecting residents or making them homeless.

Building site

The demolition progressed as normal until the last two terraces were piles of brick and rubble. The diggers moved in to start on new foundations and that is when they found it, a proper world war two bomb. A big one! Dug up in the bottom of a trench. The driver leapt out of his cab and ran across the site shouting "Bomb! Bomb!" And waving his arms to clear the area.

Dad was not panicked as he had been through all this before and made a quick recce [that's an Army term for reconnoitre] taking notes of size and any markings, although it was badly corroded. First call was to the police and within minutes sirens and blue lights surrounded us as the police taped off the streets around the site. Residents were told they had ten minutes to pack a single bag, evacuate their houses and make their way to a council run rest centre in the local drill hall.

The site was secure but a couple of Bobbies stood guard by Dad's office to stop any interlopers, reporters or concerned residents from entering the site. About an hour later, a large white truck appeared with the familiar markings of the Bomb Disposal team. I instantly recognised the Corporal who let us blow up the incendiary.

"Hi William. You won't be blowing this one up".

I hadn't really expected to because this was obviously on a whole new scale.

Dad's office was now the operations centre having access to the telephone, site plans and so on. The Superintendent of Police took charge of public order and safety while the Corporal went to recce the bomb. By the time he returned a Captain Glover, Senior Technical Officer for explosive ordnance disposal, had arrived to be briefed and take charge.

The Corporal introduced my Dad to him, "This is Sapper James Walters, Sir".

Dad interrupted,

"Ex-Sapper. I am the site manager and please call me Jimmy. Whatever you want we will do our best to provide. I guessed you want sandbags and I have my men filling them right now".

"Well done Jimmy. That's great. I guess you have done all this before".

"Once or twice" replied Dad modestly.

"Corporal Bryant believes it is a German bomb, badly corroded about five feet long and weighing 500 pounds. Please keep your men filling the sandbags while I take a look myself"

"Fred better tell your mother we are in for a long day and possibly into the night so make sure we have plenty of tea and milk and something for sandwiches. The chippy and the shops will be evacuated".

Mam and I gathered all our provisions and got the builders tea kettle bubbling away.

I was keen to get back to the action saying,

"I will tell them tea is nearly ready" and made a dash for the door before Mam could stop me, nearly knocking Captain Glover over as we arrived together.

Captain Steve Glover reported,

"We need a substantial sandbox building from sandbags to contain any potential blast. If it does go up then it will cause widespread damage".

Captain Glover discussed evacuations and cordons with the Superintendent who left to make the arrangements and check the cordons for himself.

"Jimmy. Can you get your JCB and sandbags to about thirty yards from the bomb? Gently please".

As Dad made for the door he spotted me trying to follow him,

"Fred. An army marches on its stomach so your very important job is keep everyone fed and watered".

I nodded a reluctant acceptance of my role but took satisfaction from having a vital task to fulfil.

I watched Dad drive the digger carrying a bucket full of bags and a couple of his workers riding shotgun in the cab. They repeated the trip several times until the Corporal signalled "Thumbs up" and the soldiers started the long arduous task of building a blast wall round the bomb. As he returned Mr. Clelland's Jaguar purred through the site gate with the ever-present Miss Primly at his side. He was most anxious to see that all was well and everyone including the residents were safe. Dad briefed him on the situation.

"I knew you would have it all in hand Jimmy, so nothing for me to do here. I think we will call at the rest centre and have a word with the evacuees and perhaps the local press. No point on missing some good publicity. Is there?"

Mam made the soldiers a Thermos flask of hot tea, and a pack of sandwiches and some biscuits and Dad walked them over to the sandbag pile, the soldiers waving their appreciation as they took a breather over a "Char and a wad".

In the site office, the Captain was giving a sit rep [situation report] to HQ and discussing his plan. William heard him talking about the bomb having two fuses that needed to be neutralised, hopefully in the afternoon,

"It will then take a couple of hours to soak it and make sure it's all safe before we start moving it out" he reported.

The site gates were closed to prying eyes as the soldiers unloaded a mini-tank-like machine on rubber tracks driving it into Dad's digger bucket. On his return Dad said,

"They've made a neat job of the blastwall we shall have to get them a job on the site".

Sandbox built round the bomb

Unable to contain my curiosity any longer and dragging him to one side, "Dad. Dad. What was that tank thing?" I whispered excitedly.

"It's a robot. It's a secret piece of kit and even I don't know how it works" he advised as I saw the robot disappearing into the blastbox and the heads of the soldiers working round it.

"We sit and wait now Fred. Let's grab something to eat while it's quiet".

Dad and I shared Mam's sandwiches and telling me lots about dealing with bombs and mines in the war. I was so proud of him, his bravery and his skill.

Sometime later Captain Glover returned to announce they had neutralised the fuses and the bomb was now a lot safer, but there was still a chance the explosives inside could go up. "They have started soaking the explosive out and when that is complete we will have a harmless lump of metal" he concluded confidently.

The Superintendent had now left leaving a Sergeant in charge to relay information, Dad sent the site workers home and so Mam and I were on standby with a boiling kettle and a ready supply of butties and biscuits.

It was eerily quiet. The sun was going down over the distant houses and the light from the cabin cast shadows across the site. The soldiers set up floodlights shattering the silence with the chugging of a generator.

It seemed like an eternity before Captain Glover returned.

"Jimmy, we seem to have got all the explosive out but to be on the safe side we are going to set a small controlled explosion. You never know what booby traps might have been built into the bomb. We could do with some corrugated sheets and another bucket full of sandbags to cover it if you could arrange that please".

Dad obliged and the bomb was soon safely covered and Corporal Bryant ran the cable ready to be connected to the blast machine. Captain Glover had asked the police to patrol the streets giving a warning of the explosion on their loudspeaker and a final check that all was clear to go. Mr. Clelland returned to the office to watch the show. The phone rang and the police gave the all clear. Soldiers made the last visual check of the site and Captain Glover sounded three blasts on the horn. Corporal Bryant shouted, "Firing" and plunged the handle. The bang took me by surprise being far louder than the incendiary.

"Success, I think" grinned Captain Glover. "Jimmy we may need your digger to clear up the mess and load it on our lorry if that's ok? I will give you a wave when we are ready".

The gates were opened allowing their lorry to back in and Dad set off across the site returning with a bucket full of twisted metal and debris that was quickly loaded and sheeted down on the lorry. Captain Glover thanked dad profusely for his support and cooperation and then thanked Mam and me for keeping everyone's spirits up. Corporal Bryant waved me over to the back of the lorry.

"Here you are William, a souvenir for you". Handing me a piece of twisted metal "I hope you realise just what a brave father you have there". I nodded and thanked him for my memento.

Turning to run and show Dad I stopped in my tracks on seeing him surrounded by reporters and television cameras. Mr. Clelland was spouting forth telling them what a great chap my Dad was keeping everyone safe with his prompt response to the emergency and above all his brave actions. Dad was obviously embarrassed but nodded humbly, smiled and answered their questions. Miss Primly took notes for the firm's magazine. Eventually the media circus left town, the lights appeared in the homes of the evacuees, the chippy fired up its fryers and the pub started pulling pints. All was back to normal as we locked the gates and went home to Mam.

NEW HOUSE, NEW HOME.

Dad had saved hard over the years for a deposit on a house. Mam had also put a few shillings each week into her Post Office account and when I went to school she started work part-time in a local newsagents. I had a few quid in my account which I offered but Dad said "Save it for a rainy day son. Save it for a rainy day".

They scoured the estate agents, the local papers and spent evenings touring the area for a suitable property. They looked at new houses but Dad thought they were all too small, like little boxes and not well-built. "Polly-filler villas." He called them. Eventually they came across an older property, rather rundown that had belonged to a retired doctor, recently deceased. The grounds were substantial but overgrown; the gate was rotten and falling from its hinges. Paint peeled off the windows and doors and plants lived happily in the gutters. Inside it was old fashioned, dim and musty. Some walls had oak panels with a matching picture rail. Wallpaper was drab and peeling at the corners. The kitchen had an old gas stove and boiler and a large stone sink. Overall, it was quite depressing.

Dad was more enthusiastic than Mam,

"Vee you need to imagine this house when I have refurbished it. It will be a glorious, spectacular, modern home that we will be proud of. Something we have never had".

Mam was worried about the cost and the time it would take but Dad explained he would get his trade mates to work at weekends to rewire it, plumb it, put in a boiler and central heating, new windows and doors, plaster and decorate.

"Then Vee, you can spend our moving allowance on carpet and curtains, buy a new cooker and furniture. Just think of the end result Vee".

Mam was sold on the project and by the time the building site was completed they had the house that Dad had promised, but the garden needed a lot of work. There was also a double garage and a good-sized workshop for my little business.

I remember the weekend the work inside was completed. Dad had been away at his new job and collected Mam and me from the compound to check on the new house. It did look a lot better from the outside with plant free guttering and new doors and windows. Julia called to see if I was at the house as for weeks I had spent all my free time there, often with Julia lending a hand in the workshop. The first time she came to help, she was immaculately dressed and stood out like a sore thumb. Mam found her one of my old shirts and pair of worn out school trousers destined for the rag pile. Taking a scarf, she wrapped Julia's hair up tying the scarf in a bow on her forehead.

"Not very elegant Julia but practical".

We all stood in silent admiration at what had been achieved. Dad held Mam's hand and Julia slipped her hand into mine. Suddenly there was a shriek as Dad whisked Mam off her feet and carried her through the front door,

"This is not our house Vee. This is our new home" and kissed her full on the lips.

"Oh put me down you silly devil. Not in front of the children. In any case it will be a home when I get the carpets and curtains done and put my own bits and pieces in".

Inside the house was ready to move in, fully restored and freshly decorated, new kitchen with a new-fangled eye-level grill cooker.

"No more swapping gas bottles Vee or humping coal. Just push that button". Vee did as instructed and recoiled as the boiler burst into life.

"Run the tap Fred. There should be hot water in the tank".

Sure enough, steam started to rise from the sink.

Mam in her new garden

I was enjoying Grammar School, especially the practical lessons on woodwork and technical drawing. Right up my street. I did save my money for a rainy day, but used some of it to buy hardware for new front gates and persuaded, Mr. Hooper, my woodwork teacher, to let me build the gates at school. Very kindly, he would let me in the workshop on spare periods and dinner breaks, showing me how to use the power saw and morticer. I managed to smuggle the hardware, hinges and latches and so on, in my school rucksack piece by piece but the wood was too big and heavy. Mr. Hooper came to my rescue by ordering timber direct from the wood yard. He also took me home one Friday teatime with the gates hidden in the back of his car. Mother was horrified, thinking I had been hurt or something had gone wrong and called for Dad to come and see Mr. Hooper. They looked quizzical as Mr. Hooper opened the boot for me to uncover the gates. Mam cried. I cried. Not sure about Dad but I think he was a bit teary.

"He's a credit to you Mr. Williams. An absolute delight to teach and the quality of his work is remarkable for such a youngster". Dad shook his hand still speechless while patting me on my back. Mam went to put the chettle on, yes the kettle became known as chettle after my first day at school.

That weekend Dad and I painted and hung the gates resplendent in gloss black hardware and Royal Navy Blue woodwork.

Dad worked hard making the garden look respectable uncovering many of the doctor's shrubs and bushes, mostly azaleas and rhododendrons.

"You know Vee, we deserve a housewarming party for all those who have helped us and invite the neighbours. Mam got rather worried as the guest list grew and grew.

It seemed that Mrs. Jackson was more and more curious about our new residence gently interrogating Julia for information. I don't think she ever really liked me or my relationship with Julia. It was a class thing, as I did not fit her idea of a nice boy from a good family. I only ever got as far as the front door if I called for Julia. Once, reluctantly Mrs. Jackson invited me inside when it was pouring cats and dogs and I had to stand on the mat to catch the drips. Then one afternoon Dad took me to collect Julia as we were going to the flicks in town.

Mrs. Jackson answered my knock, "She's nearly ready" she said scrutinising Dad waiting in the car. Dad waved and she managed to raise a hand limply in response. Julia was still upstairs. "Is that your father William? I didn't know he had a car" she said fishing for intelligence.

I was able to tell her in most enthusiastic fashion that it was his new company car and that he now travelled the country working from head office.

"Oh. Is he a travelling salesman?" she responded snootily.

"Certainly not. He is Regional Manager in charge of Mr. Clelland's projects".

"Really" she pondered as Julia pounded down the stairs.

Mrs. Jackson's curiosity now knew no bounds anxious to establish the extent of our social circle and intensified her interrogations on Julia's return.

"Does Mrs. Williams work?"

"She is a shop assistant like you mother".

"Yes. Yes. But we do own the shop" she emphasised. "Does Mr. Williams play golf?"

Julia told her about our housewarming and questions about the guest list came thick and fast to ascertain if anyone from her social circle was invited.

"Oh I am invited mother and I think the Mayor is going and some from the council and

Mr. Clelland his boss".

"Is the guest list closed now Julia?"

"I think Vee, Mrs. Williams is still working on it, but William and I are going to be waiting on, serving drinks and nibbles".

Julia knew her mother well and kept William fully informed,

"Mam, would it be ok to invite Julia's Mam and Dad to our housewarming?"

"Of course it would. The way your Dad keeps inviting people it seems to be the more the merrier. Here take one of these cards in an envelope. I am sure Mrs. Jackson would appreciate that" she advised, writing Mr. and Mrs. Jackson on the printed and embossed card.

Will dashed up to Julia's as planned. His knock on the door resulted in a warm smile from Mrs. Jackson and,

"Do come on in William. Nice to see you" she greeted. "How are things at home?"

"Oh all coming together very well Mrs. Jackson. The house is all done, new furniture, fitted carpet, central heating, all decorated ready for the party".

"Party William?"

Julia had appeared behind mother standing on the stairs stifling a grin.

"Oh yes Mrs. Jackson we are having a big housewarming with all sorts of bigwigs coming. Mam has asked me to give you this" pulling the envelope out of his trouser pocket.

Mrs. Jackson ran her fingers approvingly over the embossed card.

"Oh, that is most kind of your parents to invite us. We do have a busy social schedule, you know, golf club dinners and the like, but I will check our diaries and see if we are able to attend. Thank you William".

Julia and I ran off down the road laughing.

"She knows she is free because she has put "Keep clear" in her diary just in case".

Mrs. Jackson was one of the first guests to arrive for an early reconnaissance and to greet any of the bigwigs that she knew. Mr. Jackson and Dad hit it off right away with their shared interest in building and hardware. Guests rolled in thick and fast, the Mayor and Mayoress, resplendent in their chains of office, in the chauffeur-driven civic car much to Mrs. Jackson's delight, members of the chamber of trade, all dad's work mates, the neighbours who were delighted that the old doctor's house had been restored to a standard appropriate to the neighbourhood. Yes we were now posh and the presence of the town's great and good proved it.

A British Racing Green Jaguar purred up outside and I rushed out to meet Mr. Clelland and Miss Primly, though at first I barely recognised her. Off duty and socially she was a different woman, her beehive now fell in beautiful waves over her shoulders on to a black cocktail dress, lacy shoulders and a square, low-ish, but not revealing, scalloped neckline. Contact lenses replaced her spectacles but the trademark red lipstick smiled at me warmly. I could just imagine the tradesmen and many other male guests saying,

"Who is that glamour puss?" The wives may have been less enthusiastic at such competition and were keen to gossip and criticise quietly together.

"Hello, Mr. Clelland. Can I show you my latest product?" pointing to the gates. Mr. Clelland was boundless in his enthusiasm and Miss Primly said, "George, we could do with new gates".

That was first time I heard her call him George. "That's true. I will send you the measurements William and you can send me a plan and a quote". Miss Primly winked at me and I nodded my appreciation.

Mrs. Jackson was at the front of the crowd to be introduced to

Mr. Clelland and Miss Primly but she was cut off at the first fence by the Mayor and Mayoress pushing in front of her to extend a handshake to George and Joanna. Mr. Clelland was in great demand for his building services especially council projects building new council houses and there was also a plan for a new by-pass and shopping centre. No chance of Dad being short of work and a lot of the contractors wanted a piece of the action.

Julia and I circulated with drinks and canapés, that's French or posh for nibbles. Luckily grandma and granddad, now retired and sold up, had arrived a few days earlier so Grandma was busy in the kitchen saying,

"Vee you are the hostess, your job is with the guests, leave food and drink to me, your Dad and the kids".

The event was a huge success indeed it was a triumph with even Mrs. Jackson inviting Vee to one of her coffee mornings. Mr. Clelland took father's arm to one side and they disappeared into the garden. Business I assumed. There was a lot of head shaking and I thought things were getting a bit heated, but then I saw Mr. Clelland take an envelope out of his jacket pocket and force into dad's hand with a handshake, holding father's hand around the envelope. Dad seemed speechless, shaking his head as if it was something he could not believe. Mr. Clelland patted Dad on the back putting his arm around his shoulder as they returned to the house. Dad saw me watching from a distance as he pocketed the envelope and both returned smiling. He did not tell what it was all about at the time but it must have been something good. But what could be better than a new job, new car, new house and new prospects? All would be revealed.

SHENANIGANS IN THE PARK

Julia and I were not childhood sweethearts although we remained together since that first day at school. We were "just good friends". We held hands, sometimes went arm in arm but we were just good friends. We were never lovey-dovey nor did we show exaggerated affection, with frequent touching or kissing. When we met, she would run to me and give me a hug and a peck on the cheek. Nothing more. We had a circle of friends that met in the park including Archy, his girlfriend and his sister Jane, to play games or sit talking on the swings.

Jane, Archy and me

Archy and I remained very close going out together and he continued to help make products to sell and share the proceeds. I think we had finished our GCE O Level exams and had lots of extra time off school before the summer holidays. We were changing. Our bodies were changing. Teenage hormones were kicking in affecting our moods, emotions, and impulses as well as our bodies. Dark hairs started to appear under my nose, in my armpits and down below in my nether regions. Julia's body was filling out in all the right places as she metamorphosed from a young girl into a shapely young woman, like a caterpillar hatching into a beautiful butterfly.

As we lay on our backs in the park one warm and sunny afternoon I suddenly realised that I was thinking about Julia from a wholly different perspective. Was she more than just a friend? Was I feeling a different attraction to her? Were we becoming boyfriend and girlfriend? Did she feel the same way?

As I watched the fluffy white clouds traversing a clear powder blue sky I suddenly asked, "Julia. Are we boyfriend and girlfriend?"

There was a long pause and I continued to focus on the clouds not daring to look her in the eye. Julia rolled on her side, placed a hand on my cheek turning my face towards her and kissed me full on the lips, lovingly, sweetly, tenderly before lifting her face so that we were nose to nose.

"Does that answer your question?" she whispered.

"Er. Just for clarity, could you just repeat your answer" I teased.

Julia grabbed both of my cheeks and kissed me again. She snogged me hard and long, not sweetly, nor tenderly until I almost suffocated and I had to push her away and take a breath. Julia chuckled. Taking her cheeks in my hands, I drew her close to me kissing her softly on the lips and from then on, we were boyfriend and girlfriend. Julia had waited so long for me to ask the question. We were in love. In those, few precious tender moments we both realised our relationship and our world had changed and we basked silently in the warm sun pondering what the future might hold.

"Oy! You two! You can stop them shenanigans!" shattered our closest private personal meaningful moments as we looked up to see "Mr. Jobsworth" the ancient park keeper, waving his walking stick and nearly falling over as he shuffled and stumbled across the grass. Jobsworth was our nickname for him and all our gang had been the bane of his life for years by infringing his rules. We were on our feet in an instance ready to run for the park gates, but I pulled Julia towards me and kissed her again just for his benefit.

Our behaviour towards each other changed, walking with an arm on the shoulder, or round our waists were obvious signs we were closer than before. Mam noticed that her son was now taking an interest in his personal hygiene, two showers, a splash of Dad's Old Spice deodorant and clean clothes when I went out. The signals to our parents were getting clearer causing them some concern at the direction we might be going.

For our part Julia and I had no idea about our direction, in the autumn we would return to school for A Levels and then perhaps university or college. Julia was probably being lined up to enter the family business, but I had no particular idea of what lay ahead for me. We didn't talk about our personal relationship, nor marriage, having a family and all the things our parents had done in years gone by. We were just happy.

I took a lot of stick from the lads at school, most of them without girlfriends. Some boasted of having sex with lots of girls but I think it was just bravado and bragging. They all wanted to know if Julia and I had done all sorts of things to each other, things I had never heard of and they made it sound crude and vulgar. Julia had the same experience with the girls gossiping and boasting and repeating old wives tales like you cannot get pregnant standing up. We both took it all with a pinch of salt.

I was curious about the mechanics of sex, so after school I dropped in at the library.
Mrs. Ashby, the librarian had known me from a child when Mam took me in for my first Janet and John books but I don't recall that Janet and John books ever mentioned sex.
"Hello William. Anything I can help you with today?" she asked looking over her half-rimmed gold spectacles.

"Human reproduction Mrs. Ashby" I shouted in devilment.

She coughed and turned away to continue stamping her books.

The human body textbook had illustrations and even black and white photographs of male and female. The terms male and female suddenly struck a chord because times many plumbers on the building site asked me to get a three-eighths male union and a three-eighths female socket from the store. The penny finally dropped realising the male bit went inside the female bit just like a pipe joint. That was half the mystery solved, but I had yet to establish the how, when, what, where and who with aspects of sex. Did it just happen naturally one day? Was it automatic? How does one raise the idea of sex with one's girlfriend? What if she was offended? Did Julia know how to do it? Time would tell.

One Friday afternoon after school, I spent an hour on homework and then disappeared to the shower, re-appearing in fresh clothes. Once a month the Jacksons went to the golf club dinner-dance and, being a traditional ballroom event Mr. Jackson donned a black-tie dinner suit but Mrs. Jackson had a new long dress to keep up appearances.

Julia and I were left to our own devices, mostly watching the television. For several months, I slept over, in the spare room of course, conveniently located on the opposite side of the house to Julia's room. But now, the sleep over came with a veiled threat as Mrs. Jackson controlled access to "no boyfriend's land" between my room and Julia's. She made it clear she was a light sleeper and easily woken by creaking floorboards on the landing, and quickly rebuffed my offer to repair the offending floorboard saying Mr. Jackson would get round to it, "Won't you dear?"

I pictured her waiting behind her bedroom door ready to pounce on me and shove me back into my room with a broom. We did meet on the landing occasionally as she exited the bathroom festooned in curlers and her face smothered in white cream. Not a pretty sight!

As I had my tea, Mam and Dad were having an animated whispered conversation in the kitchen. I could only make out that it was a father's job emphasising quite strongly that Dad must do whatever it was promptly. Mam stood there with her arms folded, nodding in my direction. I began to fear I had done something wrong. Reluctantly Dad put down his paper and said loudly, for my benefit I think,

"Right then Vee, I had better sort that job out in the workshop."

"Will! Any chance you could give me a quick hand in the workshop?"

Something was afoot.

The workshop was empty so I was bemused as to what he wanted me to help with. Dad rocked uneasily shifting from foot to foot, coughing and clearing his throat.

"William, your Mam and I have noticed that you and Julia seem to have grown very close in the last couple of months, more like being proper boyfriend and girlfriend".

I could feel my face starting to flush with embarrassment and

Dad was looking a bit rosy and flustered as well. He seemed to be waiting for confirmation of his suspicions and he didn't have to wait long.

"Well your Mam and I want to be sure that you are being responsible and careful. You see, when a couple get together it can end badly if they are not careful".

"How do you mean being careful Dad?"

I was being mischievous guessing what he meant.

"Well sometimes the couple might have a baby and they are not married so life can be very difficult. Society, and mothers especially, expect couples to start a family when they are married because they need somewhere to live, the mother looks after the baby and father goes to work to support them, pay the rent, buy the food and so on. Having a baby is a huge commitment that changes your lives forever".

"Julia isn't pregnant" I re-assured.

"Ah well. Yes. Pleased to hear that" he stuttered, "and I wasn't suggesting she was, but you see, doing what's needed to get a baby is best left till you are married. Mam says there was a girl in Julia's class who had to leave home for a while, went to stay with her grandma they said, but she had been sent to an unmarried mother's home and the baby was adopted".

I knew about Pamela Howard because Julia befriended her when she returned to school. Pamela was no longer the bubbly lively happy girl she once was and her boyfriend finished with her. Now she was often moody and emotional breaking down into tears. She told Julia what a terrible place the home was where all the young mothers were made to feel ashamed and that it was a punishment for them being bad. Pamela told her she had no choice about the adoption, she loved her baby but the social workers and her parents forced her to sign the forms and one day the baby disappeared.

"Your Mam and I would hate to see that happen to Julia because we love her like our own daughter, so we just want you to be careful. I know girls now go on the pill but you can be careful as well" he advised, pulling a small packet marked "Durex" out of his pocket.

"Do you know about these?"

"Yes condoms. I have seen them in the barbers and we have been shown one in school".

"Well look, take these and if you need to be careful then Julia won't get pregnant but that doesn't mean you have to do anything as its always best to wait till you're older perhaps".

I took the packet from his shaking hand.

"Thanks Dad. We will be careful. Thanks for the advice".

Turning to leave the shed, I felt a deep sigh of relief from Dad and the sound of a striking match as he lit a cigarette.

I called in the kitchen for my jacket and saw Mam looking at me for a sign of how the talk had gone. I gave her a quick hug and a peck on the cheek,

"Bye Mam".

Watching me skip down the path, she must have thought she was losing her little boy, the love of her life, her pride and joy. It seemed that another female was to become the most important woman in his life.

Julia and I discussed Dad's advice.

"He is right of course Will, babies do take a lot of care, time and money and I wouldn't want to go through what Pamela Howard did. That was awful".

Mrs. Jackson avoided any such advice to her precious daughter but was forced to explain puberty when periods arrived, but in very basic terms. She did point out quite strongly that if she got too close to a boy she could have a baby, like Pamela Howard, so she should not have babies until she was married, that way she would not bring shame on the family.

"Mrs. Howard has not been the same since it got out about her Pamela" she continued.

"My advice is that you don't let a boy get too close, don't let him see you with no clothes on and don't let him touch your breasts or down there and most important sleep in separate beds, preferably in separate rooms."

We often wondered whether our parents had followed such strict terms of engagement in their courting days.

THE INTERVIEW

A Level GCE exams were finished by the end of May so we could relax from the revision and think about the next stages in our lives and our life together. Julia's parents never really sought Julia's opinion about university or a career. Girls mostly went into shops or clerical roles anyway in those days. Julia had the advantage of her father's growing business that would provide managerial opportunities and, being the only child, potentially inherit his empire. The Jacksons planned her next steps towards working in the shop and offices, getting to know the business, combined with day release to college for a business administration qualification.

Going to university was never truly considered by my parents as it had always been seen as a route to the professions, especially for the children of solicitors, doctors and vets. My grades and subjects were looking good and I did half-heartedly complete applications to a couple of universities for geography. Like many youngsters, I thought there was plenty of time left to make my mind up and I wanted to enjoy the summer and be with Julia. The thought of leaving home and being apart from Julia were also factors I wanted to ignore.

To pay my way through university, Dad got me a summer job on the nearest of his building sites under the supervision of Mr. Sewell. Suddenly the reality of life economics struck home with a vengeance; living in halls of residence then finding a house to share with a group of students, paying rent, buying food, cooking, washing up, making beds, cleaning the house, feeding the gas meter, washing my clothes, ironing them! The thought of leaving home did not appear to be an attractive proposition and appreciation for my Mam grew immensely. There would be advantages, of course; new adventures, freedom to live as I wanted, university life both academic and social, new friends, a degree and a pathway to a good career.

I was checking plans in the office when the phone rang. It was Miss Primly.

"Oh hello Miss Primly, Mr. Sewell is out on the site. Shall I call him for you or take a message?"

"No William. It is you I want to speak to. Mr. Clelland would like to see you in his office so could you make it next Thursday at 10am?" she enquired.

Taken aback and wanting to know the whys and wherefores of her request I attempted an interrogation, failing miserably as she was expert gatekeeper.

"Mr. Clelland has always taken an interest in you William and just wants a chat to see how you are getting on. Best wear a jacket and tie at head office though. See you Thursday. Don't be late. Bye for now".

Mam and Dad could not offer any explanation either but said, "Mr. Clelland moves in mysterious ways and does nothing without good reason. Best see what he wants".

The prompt to wear a collar and tie did not seem unusual, given I was visiting the boss at head office. But like Dad said I had known him most of my life and he had always been kind and generous and a fount of good advice. Perhaps I could tap this rich source for ideas about university and careers.

Tapping lightly on Miss Primly's door I saw her rise from her desk and the trademark red lipstick broke into a broad welcoming smile.

"Very smart William. My, you have grown into a proper young man".

Mr. Clelland erupted from his captain's chair greeting me halfway across his office, a firm handshake and one arm round my shoulder, he welcomed me warmly guiding me to the seat opposite at his desk.

I filled him in about life at home, and the work we had done on the house, my woodworking projects, school, A Levels, possible university, Julia's plans and so on.

He listened intently with great interest as I chatted away and my nervousness disappeared. Then he asked me a most unusual and unexpected question?

"Did you ever spend the £10 I gave you for catching that blighter Simpkins, or the £5 I paid you for the nails?"

It was like being Captain James T. Kirk on the starship U.S.S. Enterprise beaming back in time.

"They both went in the Post Office account like you advised but I have added to it and taken some out as well, so I might have spent it but made more with it" I stammered.

"Good to hear it William. That's what we call turnover, profit and loss. This company has a massive turnover, in the millions, and we need a profit to fund all the things we buy, materials and so on and, most importantly, we have a responsibility to the workforce. No profit, no wages, no work. They rely on us to feed and house their families".

"What is the map for?" I asked looking at the UK dotted with different colours.

"This is Clelland and Kirkham. Green is our current projects, yellow planned projects and red are all our suppliers. Logistics and storage are a nightmare getting materials delivered to the centre here and then re-distributed to sites".

"I often wondered why you stored so much on site because a lot was never used and then you had to dispose of it" I observed, noticing Mr. Clelland's interest.

"Go on" he said.

"Car makers are now using JIT, J.I.T, just in time. They get the suppliers to deliver what they need directly to the production line so no logistics and no storage. The suppliers make many components off site and I wondered if the building industry could do the same. Instead of building a roof from a bale of timber, why not have trusses made in a factory and delivered on demand?" I sounded very innovative and forward thinking but owed my newfound knowledge to a technical magazine at school.

Mr. Clelland seemed stunned and pensive as he jotted notes on his pad. This is the kind of thinking needed in our company William. We are bound by the old ways. If we are to survive and be competitive we must change and keep ahead of the competition".

Smiling benignly he said, "Have a look round William. Do you recognise anything?"

Scanning the walls I saw pictures of Mr. Clelland and his partner, Bill Kirkham on some of their projects, some shaking hands with hobnobs and even royalty. My eyes fell on a display cabinet containing numerous silver presentation trowels from topping out ceremonies. In the centre was a National Dried Milk tin and I ran over to check it out. It was empty apart from my original handwritten invoice.

"Is this my......." but before I could finish Mr. Cleland said,

"Yes William it is one of your tins of nails. I keep it as a memento and a reminder of how I started my working life with nothing more than my hands as an apprentice joiner. I value that tin more than anything else you see here".

"Anyway young man down to business....."

We discussed various options; university, building trades, apprenticeships, life with Julia, getting married and starting a family.

"Have you ever considered the skills and life experiences you can offer an employer?"

I struggled to list more than my academic achievements to date, a hard worker, good with plans and woodworking, reminding Mr. Clelland of the gates I built for him.

That's only a start William. Let me tell you how I see you given I have known you since a boy. You have great technical ability with plans and joiner's rods, a good joiner but not qualified, good financial sense in a small way, but your actions on the site showed me how to minimise waste and costs. You have an intimate knowledge of building materials and how things are put together. If I was interviewing a university graduate now for a job he would not know the ratios of sand and cement, how to measure and cut a bird mouth and work out the angles for rafters. He would know a lot of other things he had learnt in theory but what he would not know William is how things work on a site, how to deal with the workmen, tricks of the trade good and bad. Above all he would not know how to communicate with them".

I started to realise where all this going. He was describing my life.

"Unless he was from Scotland he wouldn't know any Glaswegian" I chimed in.

"Exactly William. Now you see my point. You have a significant advantage over the graduate. It took you years to gain such an experience and the graduate has had three years learning theory at university. All you need is some time in college to supplement your wealth of knowledge, especially in building site languages" he chuckled.

There was silence as his words echoed round my brain making links with thousands upon thousands of little life events that may have been meaningless then but now the brain was pulling them together from long forgotten data files to create a picture of a young man with a lot to offer.

"I am beginning to understand where you are coming from Mr. Clelland but I am not sure where all this is going".

"I am offering you a job William. Not just a job but also a great opportunity to be a qualified professional, a job for life, good rewards to finance a comfortable life together with Julia, a nice house for your family if you want one, a chance to see the world at work and foreign holidays. I strongly believe William you have the ability and experience to be a Quantity Surveyor".

I must have looked rather vacant although I had come across one or two on site.

Mr.Clelland explained that a Quantity Surveyors managed all costs on building and civil engineering projects, from the initial calculations to the final figures, enhanced value for money, met legal standards and ensured statutory building regulations are met, finally create reports to show profitability.

I know William you have the desired abilities, good maths especially in a construction environment, attention to detail, able to analyse problems and solutions, you will learn a greater understanding of engineering science and technology and knowledge of building and construction. I have seen over the years you are able to use your initiative and take the right courses of action".

There was a further long ponderous moment as I reflected on whether he was talking about William Walters, Fred from the building site".

"So William I am offering you an apprenticeship as a quantity surveyor, working in head office and on site, with day release for college to get your qualification, a good wage and fantastic prospects with this company. Just look how your father has progressed with us. He was just as speechless when I offered the job as Regional Manager but he said yes. Will you say yes William?"

"It's a lot to take in Mr. Clelland and such a complete surprise. You have opened my eyes to what I am and what I could be and I thank you for that. I think my answer would be yes. Dare I ask what the starting salary is please?"

Mr. Clelland smiled, opening a brown folder on his desk to reveal my contract, pointing at a space next to salary with a figure pencilled in".

"A wise man advised me in business not to take the first offer and I should negotiate for the best price to sell or buy. I have been enlightened today as to the scope and extent of my qualities and potential, so I think an extra £500 a year would be acceptable. On your part you will have a trusted employee committed to your company."

I don't know where that all came from or where I got the courage to seek an extra £500.

Mr. Clelland never batted an eyelid. Just as he did with Dad, he fixed his gaze on me as I spoke, watching my every movement. Standing up he offered his hand over the desk.

"Done. I shall have to be more careful with advice in future" he laughed.

"What are doing between now and September?"

"I planned to work on the site to pay my way to university that's all".

"Can I suggest you take the summer off, perhaps with Julia, and go and see some of the world. I see a lot of students come out of university and go backpacking for a year. I'm not suggesting you do that but travel across Europe go and look at some of the great buildings ancient and modern, Notre Dame, Eiffel Tower, Gaudi's unfinished cathedral in Barcelona, see what the French and Germans have achieved rebuilding their cities and infrastructure, see how the Dutch have reclaimed land from the sea. Above all, look how Europe is developing their common market. This company needs to be part of that. Don't spend all your time looking at buildings or else Julia will be really fed up. See the sights. Enjoy the Mediterranean, the food, the wine, the culture and their way of life" he enthused.

"Phew. That's a lot to take in and sounds fantastic but I am not sure Mrs. Jackson will let us go together if you know what I mean and I am not sure my Post Office account will run to that, especially if Julia comes as well".

"You are quite capable of planning such a trip and I have a few contacts over there who will be pleased to show you the sights. Tell Mrs. Jackson you will have separate bedrooms" he chuckled.

"As for finance, well, be guided by Wilkins Micawber from David Copperfield who was always optimistic that something would turn up. Miss Primly will alter the contract and send it to you as I am sure you will want to discuss it with Vee and Jimmy and Julia, of course."

Mr Clelland pressed a button on his intercom and Miss Primly appeared promptly. Joanna, our William is considering an apprenticeship with us. Please amend his salary details" and handed her the file.

"If you hang on William I can give you your contact to save posting" and took another file from her desk. It already stated the salary increase he had negotiated. "He thought you might try to better his offer".

William held out his hand to Miss Primly who took him by the shoulders and plonked a bright red kiss on his cheek. If only the boys on the building site could have seen that.

Not surprisingly Dad was home from work early, anxious to hear what the meeting was all about. Mam was playing it cool as if she knew nothing about my visit to head office. But a warm hug and a Victoria sponge with fresh cream indicated they had an inkling. I tucked into the cake and a mug of builder's tea as they watched and waited for some news. They asked a few exploratory questions like "How was Mr. Clelland?" "Did you see Miss Primly?" "What did I think to head office?"

I batted off attempts to extract the details from me but eventually I just said,

"He offered me an apprenticeship. That's all".

The questions flew thick and fast and my answers grew more and enthusiastic revealing my joy and happiness at the opportunity. Both were delighted.

"You said Mr. Clelland moved in mysterious ways".

I then moved on to his idea of a European tour with Julia. I have to say neither were taken aback at the idea and it probably was not appropriate to raise the subject of "being careful" and separate bedrooms. I was more concerned with the cost and told them what Mr. Clelland said about Wilkins Micawber, that something would turn up.

"He may be right Fred. You won't need funds for university and you will be earning a good wage as soon as you return. I am sure we can work something out financially".

My next move was to see Julia who was delighted that I would be at home. Jobsworth was nowhere in sight so she gave me a hug, kissing me on the cheek.

"What is this red mark on your cheek? she queried suspiciously.

"Oh I can explain that" I stuttered.

"It looks like lipstick to me William Walters. Start explaining".

She was as surprised as I was that Miss Primly had planted one on my cheek.

"It was a complete surprise but it wasn't like a girlfriend kiss it was more like a sister or mother kiss".

Julia seemed to accept the truth and polished the stain from my cheek with her hankie. "There. That's got rid of the other woman in your life" she chided with a chuckle. "You are all mine again".

Crisis averted, I went on to describe Mr. Clelland's plan to tour Europe together. I thought Julia might dismiss it out of hand, as she had never struck me as being very adventurous. Neither was I for that matter, as the opportunity had never arisen, nor the funds been available, but people were now going on package tours to the continent for sun, sand, sea and the other.

"Somehow we have to get this past your mother and find the cash".

The following Saturday evening Mam organised a dinner party

at home, for Archy and his parents and the Jacksons. Archy was set to go to university to study chemistry and then onward into industry. The menu was typical of the time, Seafood cocktail, brown bread and butter triangles; Duck a L'orange and Pineapple Upside Down Cake. I noticed eleven starters ready to serve on the kitchen table.

"Oh I always make extra just in case of accidents."

My suspicions were soon answered as a new bright red Jaguar rolled up the drive with

Mr. Clelland at the wheel. Joanna sported an equally bright red lipstick matching the colour of the car and just as glossy.

There followed warm welcoming handshakes and introductions and, Mrs. Jackson was in her element in the presence of near royalty. "Oh please. Call me Janice. Mrs. Jackson seems so formal" she advised in her poshest accent.

We sat down to our starter and glasses of Mateus Rose which seemed to get the conversation flowing freely. Julia had asked me what the party was all about but I could not explain especially now that The Clellands had been invited and the single large diamond on Miss Primly's finger proved to be part of the celebrations.

Mam sat opposite to Joanna giving her the opportunity to keep glancing at the diamond on Joanna's finger. Eventually their eyes met and Mam nodded subtly towards the ring raising her eyebrows to silently ask the question. Joanna nodded her response.

"Would everyone like coffee?" asked Mam.

"I will come and help you" offered Joanna, seizing the opportunity to reveal her news.

In the kitchen Mam took hold of Joanna's left hand to admire the ring.

"Our relationship was always the worst kept secret, living together all these years. We were never blessed with children, so for us there was no need to marry, we were happy as we were, apart from George calling me 'Joa er Miss Primley'. George wanted to ensure that if he was to die before me there would be no legal issues with inheritance, hence we are engaged to be married".

Mam and Joanna hugged.

"George and I love children; you see what he has been like with William over the years. It would be our greatest wish and a privilege, if we could be adopted as honorary grandparents".

Mam threw her arms open wide then wrapping them round Joanna, they waltzed round the kitchen in a tight embrace, laughing and crying at the same time.

Recovering their decorum and repairing their tear stained faces the ladies returned to the dining room and served the coffee. George sensed something had been going on in the kitchen and looked at Joanna for a sign, as she placed a cup in front of her fiancé and, bending forward whispered,

"Your coffee Granddad."

Joanna walked behind his chair gently stroking her hand across his shoulders, as George spun round, his facial expression pleading for confirmation. She nodded and smiled gleefully.

George's whole body was ready to explode with joy and happiness.

"Vee. Can I say that dinner was most enjoyable and quite continental. Does this whet your appetite William to see Europe?" he enquired, starting to move in one of his mysterious ways.

"Janice what do you think about William's apprenticeship to the profession of Quantity Surveyor. Don't you think it is such a marvellous opportunity?"

"Oh absolutely George" she agreed, rather squiffy, particularly approving the word profession.

"I have suggested that he and Julia should travel to Europe on a working holiday, see the sights and get an understanding of what the European Union is all about. I see it as the future. Not just for Clelland and Kirkham but all businesses. Don't you agree Brian?"

Directing his question to Mr. Jackson who launched into a detailed approval of the concept.

"What about you Janice don't you agree with me that it would be of great benefit to these two young sensible responsible people to see more of the world? We never had the opportunity did we?"

Janice nearly choked on her Mateus Rose for she was now bottled up in a corner and struggled to cough and splutter positively to the idea. She was about to clear her throat and raise the issue of funding but Mr. Clelland cut her off at the pass.

Rising to his feet he proclaimed,

"Several years ago these two boys, William and Archiy thwarted a plot to rob my company. They showed great courage and quick-thinking leading to the arrest of four armed criminals from London and they are still in prison now I believe. This gang also robbed another of my building sites two years before using the same Modus Operandi, demolishing a bollard to create an escape route. They were never caught but the actions of these two boys led to them being convicted for that robbery as well".

Everyone was enthralled as he continued.

"The insurance company offered a reward for information leading to the capture of the gang but they would not pay that reward to my company. However, they did pay it to those responsible for the arrest provided it was invested in a trust until they were eighteen years of age. When Jimmy and Vee moved into this house, I gave Jimmy the papers and now is the time to reveal how that investment has grown...... Jimmy".

Dad removed two envelopes from his suit pocket handing one to Archibald Armour and the other to myself. This was all unbelievable. Incredible. I could barely move let alone slit the envelop open. Archy beat me to it screaming with disbelief and delight at the contents. Julia handed me her butter knife and we joined in with Archy's celebrations. The Armours and the Jacksons were stunned as they read the number of zeros on the cheque.

"Wilkins Micawber was right William. Something did turn up".

PHOTOGRAPHS

Unless otherwise stated photographs come from the author's family collections.

Other contributors are:

NARPO Derbyshire

Norfolk Police

Public domain

Cover picture
Construction Site, Belfast geograph-6825367-by-Rossographer

York Station, with a London Midland train in the North Eastern Region Capital
cc-by-sa/2.0 - © Ben Brooksbank - geograph.org.uk/p/2057091

Suncourt Enclosure, Scarborough
cc-by-sa/2.0 - © Paul Harrop - geograph.org.uk/p/4520418

'Prefab' housing.
cc-by-sa/2.0 - © Paul Eggleston - geograph.org.uk/p/389577

Demolition, Bangor

cc-by-sa/2.0Â - Â©Â RossographerÂ -Â geograph.org.uk/p/3405087

The Crooked Spire cc-by-sa/2.0 - Â© David Martin geograph.org.uk/p/3922775

ABOUT THE AUTHOR

Charlie Parkes

My brain and I have been together for over 70 years achieving some remarkable things and some dismal failures! Measure once - cut once – buy another worktop, for example! These days I do find it harder to deal with irrelevant data. All I need is the bottom line. If I want more data, I will ask for it or Google it, or just switch off from my loved ones. I can be forgetful and find it hard to recall things but that is normal and does not mean that I am losing my marbles. Indeed, I have a full tin on my bookshelf. I know that my brain has filed huge amounts of data unconsciously and it just takes a bit longer tracking it down. It is all in there somewhere! However, it is difficult to find what you do not know the brain has stored for a rainy day and there is no index or search engine!

Suddenly, something pops into my consciousness and I wonder, "Where did that come from? What triggered that thought? And why?"

As founder of Swanwick Men's Shed, I have observed various

forms of Alzheimer's and dementia at close hand and fear the onset of these debilitating conditions in my old age. It is terribly sad to see skilled woodworkers unable to recognise the tools and machinery they once used to create masterpieces in wood. I have also seen how people have regained the ability to enjoy life as a member of the shed. For some it has been a lifesaver. For a bereaved member the shed becomes their family. To offset dementia I keep The Times General Knowledge crossword books dotted round the house to dip in to, as and when. It is a comfort to find that my brain function improves with practice but I also find them rather soporific.

I also find that instinctively shooting clay pigeons on a fast and furious drive proves that my brain, eye and body can still coordinate. My motto is "Still shooting. Still living." Over many years, I have written books on countryside law and conservation. Getting every comma and full stop correct in a legal text is pretty tedious and tiresome stuff. In 1996, I wrote a small book of Shaggy Dog Stories that was purely fictional and imaginative and great fun to do. I relished the freedom to write without constriction. The title and some of the tales hark back to stories told by my father from his army days, and I enjoyed embellishing them with detail based upon characters I developed from friends and family.

I truly enjoy visualising a location or a character and describing them with a picture in words. Imagination gives you the freedom to create your own characters and personalities. They are the actors in your theatre bringing your words, actions and locations to life to entertain an audience. In your imagination, you can do anything thought to be impossible. The story line can take over all my waking thoughts and I jot down notes, wherever I am, and rush home to type them up. Never let an idea get away as you may not find it again. Imagination can take you wherever you want in the world at any time in history, or the future, even to places that do not exist. I find the mental process invigorating and exciting and realise that the old brain is not dead or dying! Being creative has been a hugely enjoyable, fun and rewarding experience leaving the brain energised as if it was on fire. Creative writing is a great exercise for the brain - all you need is a spark. As Jane Austen said, "Indulge your imagination in every possible flight." [Pride and Prejudice.] You do not need to publish just try short stories or your life story. No need for them to be fiction either, just write about what you know or have done.

In 2015, I took my wife on a railway holiday on the West Highland Line and Hogwarts Express. On the bleak and rain swept misty Rannoch Moor I saw a young woman leave the train and disappear into the mist. I began to imagine what might befall her alone in the boggy wilderness. I told my "sister" Carla and fifteen years later found a spark of an idea that fired the imagination for a romantic mystery novel about The Hidden Glen in the Scottish Highlands, published in her name on Amazon as an EBook and paperback. Rudyard Kipling, the author, not the cake-maker said, "I keep six honest serving-men (They taught me all I knew); their names are What and Why and When and How and Where and Who. Choose a person, a location or situation, apply the 5Ws and you are up are running. The data is all in that brain of yours somewhere.

Shaggy Dog Stories – Tales of the Countryside 2023
I published Shaggy Dog Stories in 1996 selling over 10,000 copies. With only two copies left on my shelf, I decided it was time to republish and search my brain for some new material. I found one hundred percent more new stories and published on Amazon in 2023. The new edition consists of thirty-two stories illustrated with line drawings and featuring Spot the beer-drinking, domino-playing shaggy dog who pops up throughout the book to prove that man is a dog's best friend!

The Hidden Glen Carla Parkes 2019
It's Fresher's Week at Portsmouth University and Emma is thrown into the melting pot that independent life and university bring.

She befriends three girls from different backgrounds and levels in society. Perhaps these innocents abroad were attracted to each other by their common denominator – being insular, not worldly wise, not streetwise. but together they would look to each other and after each other in a lasting friendship.

Explore Emma's childhood, her "Uni" friends, the men in her life, her sailing and rambling adventures from Scotland to the south coast, France, Italy and the Peak District. Through difficult, emotional times, she is guided by the wisdom of her wonderfully philosophical "Nannee Jane" who always finds positive outcomes on her encounters. rather like Jane Austen. Is there a link between Nannee Jane and Jane Austen apart from family connections with Chawton? Following several false starts and one disturbing end to a relationship, Emma continues her quest to find her perfect man.

Hoping for peace and solitude away from nine-to-five in a London fashion house, she embarks on a lone, wild-walking, trek in the Scottish highlands where she meets a mysterious fellow traveller in a remote fishing hut. The events that follow in the Hidden Glen remain unfathomable, magical, mystical and beyond all human reasoning. Emma returns to her family and university friends where she reveals almost all her secrets.

Several years later Emma retraces her steps, but this time she is not alone, in a quest to find the man, love and the happiness she left behind in the Hidden Glen.

Discover whether she unravels the mysteries of the glen and if there is a potential return to reality for the lovers.

Illuminated with Jane Austen quotations about love, marriage and happiness as relevant now as the day she wrote them. Lavishly illustrated with photographs so you can walk in Emma's footsteps or even visit all the locations except, that is, for the Hidden Glen.

Law Of The Countryside A handbook for the Countryside Management Association 1980

Fair Game – The Law Of Country Sports And The Protection Of Wildlife [Co-Author John Thornley OBE]

1987 Deer: Law And Liabilities [Co-Author John Thornley OBE] - 2000

Printed in Great Britain
by Amazon